Slippers & Chains
Sugar Dust

Raven ShadowHawk

little
vamppress

Slippers & Chains:
Sugar Dust

Published in July 2015 by Little Vamp Press

Cover design: 'ravenink'
Editor: Jennifer Harrington

All characters and words the work of Raven ShadowHawk

All characters, locations, names or incidents appearing in
this work are fictitious and a product of the author's
overactive imagination. Resemblance to any real persons,
living, dead, vampire, ghost, zombie, lycanthrope, faerie or
daemon is purely coincidental. Promise.

This book is sexually graphic and intended for a mature
audience. This book, and others in the series, should only be
purchased and/or read by those for whom it is legal,
according to the laws in their country of residence.

THE HISTORY OF SUGAR DUST

'Sugar Dust' is my first novella to be picked up by a publisher.

Breathless Press took me on as one of their authors in June 2014 and invited me to become part of their kind, generous and loving family.

In May 2015 Breathless Press closed its doors, marking the end to the many years of quality erotica and romance they were known for.

While I'm sad that Breathless Press has closed, I'm grateful because I learned a great deal in my time with them. I will forever remember their kindness, professionalism and, above all, their dedication to ensuring that all authors on their staff were treated fairly and respectfully.

You, BP, are an example of what all publishers should be. I'll miss you terribly.

ACKNOWLEDGEMENTS

Special thanks must go out to Jenn, my editor, who took this novel when I thought it was done and helped me turn it into something spectacular! I'm saddened that we'll no longer be working together but I'll never forget the work we did and how much I learned through collaborating with you.

David Soden (my Funk Master!) who gave me the nudge (then the shove!) I needed when unsure if anybody would care about a 'normal' BDSM relationship following the popularity of a certain trilogy that shall remain nameless. His unerring support, quiet pride and humorous take on what constitutes 'normal' is a good portion of why this book is in your hands today.

Members of the Phoenix Writers Group . . . you should be proud of yourselves! Your enthusiasm for 'The Cage Story' has led to a novella that I hope will delight and amuse others as much as it did you.

DEDICATION

To everyone at Breathless Press.
This wouldn't be if not for you . . .

KAREN

Karen tried to kneel taller, but succeeded only in knocking her head against the top of the four-foot cage. Hair cushioned the blow, but the sensory echo of the impact lingered along the top of her skull for long seconds afterwards. The physical reminder of her captivity and helplessness sent tingles racing from her toes to the tips of her fingers. Her heart fluttered.

I can't wait much longer. I'll explode if he doesn't touch me . . .

Pulling her sore knees to her chest, she peered through the thick, metal bars. 'Please.' The begging note in her voice gave her the verbal weight of a ten-year-old.

Brown eyes gleaming, one hand massaging his crotch, Dan stalked closer. A slim lock of hair tumbled over his forehead like a curl of salt and pepper silk. A sharp toss of his head flicked it back and showcased the subtle ripple of muscles across his neck and shoulders. 'Please, what?'

'Please, Sir, let me come.'

'No.'

She whimpered at his deadpan tone. Frustration fired up her blood and mingled with the thrill over his control. His denial of her need. His absolute power.

'You need to earn it.' He unfastened the top button of his jeans and gave a wide smile. That smirk spoke of wicked pleasures, a language Karen knew well. She yearned to cross her legs to give pressure to the delicate button high between her thighs that throbbed at the thought of *earning* her reward.

'Come here,' he murmured.

Obedient and eager, Karen lowered her knees and clumsily rocked herself into a kneeling position. It took several tries with the spreader bar between her ankles. She had added difficulty with her wrists chained at the small of her back; her hands were of no use. The chain from the handcuffs pooled on the small of her back then slipped down the crack of her arse. Its metallic touch tickled like a cold, teasing finger. She shivered and sucked a deep breath through her open mouth. She reached back, fumbling for the bars of the cage. Pain spasmed across her overextended shoulders. Her fingernails scraped Dan's thigh.

'I can't reach like this,' she whined.

'Why bother with all that yoga if you can't bend a bit?'

'Screw you.'

'You wish.' His eyes narrowed. The look stole the breath from her lungs. He wouldn't really leave her hanging would he?

Dan's voice roughened as he ordered, 'Try harder.'

Karen strained until her shoulders shrieked for mercy and her fingers found the coarse curls of Dan's pubic hair. She yanked a few strands, winding them around her finger in tightening coils.

'Hey,' he yelped. 'None of that.'

'It's difficult when I can't see.' She bit her lip, hoping her lowered eyes and soft voice would work as well here as those times when she conveniently *forgot* to wash the dishes after dinner. 'I didn't mean it.'

'Bullshit. Get over to the other side. I want your mouth.'

The words sent another pulse of pleasure through her stomach. A trickle of moisture oozed from her hypersensitive pussy lips, warm and slick on her skin. Smirking, she shimmied over and met Dan in the far corner. He dropped his trousers on the way around. With a slight grunt he kicked off his boxers and stood before her naked.

Karen froze, mesmerised by the sight of his skin. It was unblemished and perfect except for the faint red lines across his thighs and knees, all angled towards the juncture of his legs. Her fingertips itched to touch him again and to add more nail marks to the fading collection.

He pressed his hips to the side of the cage, and whispered, 'Suck me.'

Extending her tongue, Karen licked a glistening, pearly smear from the tip of his cock then closed her mouth around him. The warmth of him, the salty muskiness made her moan.

She wished her hands were tied in front.

He groaned and began to thrust, long, slow motions that occasionally stroked the back of her throat. 'Good girl, Kaz. Just stay there.'

She longed to suck him in and never let go. Breathless need consumed her. She braced herself. His hot length slid deeper.

The phone rang.

Karen flinched, but Dan continued thrusting, eyes closed as if to shut out the intrusion. Three seconds after the ringtone stopped, it rang again.

'Oh, come on,' he roared.

Karen arched one eyebrow and flexed her jaw as he pulled away. His expression in that moment reminded her of their first months together and the disappointment in his gaze each time she left his bed. She watched him snatch his mobile off the dresser and wondered when exactly he'd stopped reaching for her body in such an eager and passionate way.

'What?' he snapped. 'Sorry, I . . . no, Mum, of course I'm glad to hear from you.'

Sighing, Karen sat down and leaned in the corner. She extended her wide-spread legs before her. With her eyes closed, she prepared for the emotional hurricane otherwise known as Maxine Scotney.

'I'm great, thanks. Just spending some time with Karen— yes, *the one with the afro.*' He grimaced.

The apologetic look he shot her way only fanned the flame of irritation. Why couldn't he – wouldn't he – defend her? Why did he always have to be so weak?

'My girlfriend,' Dan continued, pacing around the cage in a large circuit which included the bed against the far wall,

3

the bookcase and drawers opposite, and the wardrobe on the right.

Karen watched him move and gnawed her lower lip. Still naked, his body drew her eye like paperclips to a desk magnet. She drank in his strong strides and narrow hips with a slight paunch around the belly button and remembered his pleasure as he gobbled down the latest of her "experimental" dinners.

The memory of his praise and rewarding caresses almost made her forget who was on the other end of the phone. Then the whine in Dan's voice dragged her back.

'I'm in the middle of something right now. Yes, she's here with me.'

Karen tensed and drummed her fingers against bars. 'Tell her to get lost!' she said, in a half lowered voice.

Dan placed his index finger against his lips. His eyebrows knitted almost into one.

She hated being shushed.

Her body ached. Left over promises of pleasure still tingled along her flesh. Yet again, she wished her hands were tied in front. She lifted her knees and rubbed her breasts against her thighs, the friction offering minimal relief to the tightening nubs of her nipples.

Above the chest of drawers, the wall clock marked each stolen second of play with a doleful click.

Dan scrubbed his hands through his hair. 'Mum, this isn't a good time.'

'You're right. We're meant to be playing.' This time when she spoke, she didn't bother to lower her voice. Something inside her gut warmed at the thought that Maxine might hear that her presence was unwanted. It might finally force Dan to tell her where she stood.

Dan slapped the handset against his chest and raised a finger in warning, the playful look of moments ago, replaced with a furrowed brow and eyes dark with worry.

His expression freed a wave of shame within her that swelled and swallowed her pleasure. It left Karen cold and uncomfortable, shifting against her restraints. When the chains jangled against the cage bars she froze.

Dan glanced at his watch. 'That's twenty minutes away. Why didn't you call sooner?' He waited. His shoulders slumped. 'I'll come get you.'

Karen sat upright and her mouth hung open. Before she could object, Dan hung up. She stared at him, abruptly aware of her harsh breathing. 'What the hell?' An involuntary spasm twitched through her hands and she fought to keep them steady. The battle was lost before it began. The warmth of anger replaced that of pleasure.

'Mum and Dad are on a train. They're already at Market Harborough now.'

'We're a bit busy.' Rolling her eyes, she jangled the handcuff chains. 'Can't they get a bus? Or a cab?'

He avoided her gaze, staring at the corner of the cage. 'You know what Mum's like.'

Another eye roll. Of course she knew, but did he?

She steadied herself with a soft breath then spoke in a low, calm voice. 'Did you know they were coming?'

'No.' Dan reached into the cage bars and stroked her head. Before she could enjoy the sensation, he pulled away and retrieved his boxers. 'I have no idea what she wants, but it's better if I just go.'

Karen ached to shake him. She wanted to grab his shoulders and shriek in his face like a deranged harpy. Instead she glared at the floor. 'It's been weeks since I had you to myself. Why does she have to spoil this?'

'What about Monday?'

She thought back to the sweaty tangle of bodies earlier in the week. She recalled the sensation of many hands gliding over her skin and the insistent thrust of a tongue in her mouth while another lapped her clit. Though the memory filled her belly with threads of heat, she shook her head. 'I said *myself*. I don't want to share with the rest of your Library every time we play.'

He pulled on his trousers and gave a lop-sided grin. 'Come on, you loved it. Hannah and Rebecca did too.'

Karen risked meeting his eyes. Though several responses came to mind, none of them fit the whirlwind of frustration and anger tearing through her mind. 'I'm sure they did,' she said at last, 'but why is it always us *and* someone else?'

'It's fun.'

'Yes, but—'

'What's the problem? It's not like you don't benefit from my Slave Library.' Dan searched the floor, picking his way through the plethora of toys. 'All those pretty women . . .'

'What are you doing?'

'I need the key,' he sighed. 'You need to get dressed.' His shoulders slumped and "Dan The Dom" left the room. Playtime was over.

Karen made one last attempt to coax him back. 'Don't you want your mum and dad to see me in your favorite outfit?' She smiled and kicked out until the spreader bar clanged against the bars. 'You never know, they might like it.'

He chuckled. 'I should spank you.'

'Do . . . I'm begging.'

Dan picked up a coil of rope and ran it through his fingers before tossing it on the bed. After scanning the floor one more time he put his hands on his hips. 'Shit,' he hissed.

'What now?' She knew that look and tone of his voice. 'They don't want to stay the night too, do they?'

'Yes, but remember we used to joke about you living in the cage on soup?'

Karen snorted. 'Messing with my food is a hard limit, Sir.'

A frown wrinkled his brow. 'I can't find the cage key.'

'Where's the spare?'

'I'm not sure.'

A bead of sweat trickled down Karen's spine. 'How can you not be sure?'

'It used to be in that cup on the dresser, now it's not.'

'How the hell do I get out?'

Dan tapped his chin. Then, as he tugged on a shirt he said, 'I have an idea.' He snatched up his phone and swiped the screen with his thumb. 'Stay there.' He left the room, calling over his shoulder.

'Ha-bloody-ha.'

Karen slumped. The fading thrill of being controlled, trapped, and restrained left her cold. Without Dan's warm hands or the promise of his attention, the sensation of cuffs around her wrists went from sexy to irritating. The collar around her neck chafed her skin. The ache in her overstretched thighs crawled up to encompass her hips.

A rumble from the heater reminded her she wore nothing but leather and metal. She shuffled toward the side nearest the jets of warmth.

When Dan returned, he wore a jacket and shoes.

'Dan, please don't leave me.'

'I have to pick them up.'

'What about me?' Karen clenched her fists. 'You don't have to run every time mummy calls. You're not her baby anymore.'

His eyes narrowed. 'Steady, Kaz.'

'Look at me! I'm naked . . . wearing a spreader bar . . . in a cage.' She twisted against the bars. 'What do you think she'll say when she sees me?'

'She won't. Pete's coming.'

She shrugged. 'And what's he supposed to do about this?'

'He'll find the key.'

'And you?'

'I have to go.' He stood in front of the cage and slid a hand through the bars. 'I'm sorry.'

Karen jerked away, unwilling to let his gentle touch fog her thinking. Not this time.

'Don't be like that.'

'What do you want me to say? "I'm fine in here naked while you pick up your folks?" No way. At least uncuff my hands and legs.'

Dan glanced at his watch again. Sighing, he plucked a single small key from the dresser and slotted it through the bars into her hand. 'Here, I've got to go.' He darted from the room.

Karen winced. Her body shook, though not with cold.

'I hate you right now,' she called.

'I'll make it up to you later.' He voice floated back to her, muffled by several walls.

Yeah, right. But first you need to be here.

She sighed and tossed her head back, clenching and unclenching her fingers. Then Karen shut her eyes and concentrated on unlocking the cuffs by feel. The key slipped around the lock for several seconds before sliding from her numb fingers. It hit the floor, bounced, and then sailed through the bars of the cage and beneath the chest of drawers.

'No, no, no!' She wiggled round and craned her neck just enough to see the faint gleam of silver amongst the clumps of dust and empty condom wrappers.

Goosebumps prickled up her arms and thighs. She opened her mouth to call out and heard the front door slam. Silence descended on the house.

'Fuck!'

DAN

'Darling, where are you?'

Dan ground his teeth as the voice filled his ear. His fingers flexed on the steering wheel and tightened until his knuckles whitened. As the traffic crawled forward another inch, he saw the miniature titan that was his mother in his mind's eye. Wagging her finger at him.

'Queen's Road, Mum.'

A soft sigh came from the Bluetooth receiver. 'Miles away. Why didn't you leave sooner?'

'You're here, then?'

'Your father and I have been standing here like vagrants for five whole minutes. You should have left sooner.'

'And *you* could have called sooner.' He jabbed a finger at the air, imagining his mother's face in its place.

'Don't be so grumpy, darling. We're here to see you.'

'Sorry,' he said in his most saccharine tone. 'You could take a bus if you don't want to wait. It's cheaper than a cab. The stop is right outside the station.' Hope filled his voice.

'Ugh, no thank you. The train was bad enough. Just hurry along, darling.'

He hung up and jumped when the phone immediately rang again, the tone transferred to the receiver in his ear.

'What?' He snapped when the call connected.

'Sorry, mate, I just— where's your spare key?'

Some of the stiffness eased out of Dan's shoulders. 'Pete, thank God. You're there?'

'Yeah, but I don't see the key.'

'Inside a fake rock under the rose bush.'

Several tense seconds passed. Dan heard his friend wrestling with the bush and the sharp yelp meaning he'd probably found a number of thorns.

'Got it,' he said.

Dan closed his eyes. He took a brief moment to enjoy the lightness as some of the tension seeped from his shoulders. 'Okay, and Pete? When you get in there . . . be sensitive, okay?'

'Eh?'

'Karen's likely to be pissed off.' He licked his lips. 'Try not to make it worse.'

A long pause followed. 'What's going on?'

'I wouldn't have called you if I wasn't desperate. Tell her that.'

For the fourth time since dashing off in the car he struggled to think of an alternative scenario. One that kept both his mother and girlfriend happy, and him with a full set of functioning body parts. Still no luck.

'Mate, what have you done?'

'I need to go.' Heat crept up his neck and jaw. Dan hung up. He removed the Bluetooth headset, put the phone on silent and tried to concentrate on the road ahead instead of what Pete would soon uncover in his bedroom. Again he thought of Karen's face when he left her; brows scrunched, down turned lips and a deep sadness in her eyes. His own chest ached at leaving her that way, but what choice did he have?

Ten minutes and six missed calls later, Dan pulled into the train station car park and stopped in front of a tiny, silver haired woman waving an equally tiny hankie. Her dress, reminiscent of some garish seventies curtain, billowed in the breeze and displayed an unwelcome length of leg encased in nylon.

'Darling!' she cried. 'I thought you'd never get here.'

The sound of that crisp, nasal voice sapped all the righteous rage Dan had managed to cultivate on the car ride over. The voice dragged him back twenty years, maybe even thirty, and placed him at his mother's side, hanging his head as she brandished yet another of his second place trophies.

'It *is* rush hour, Mum.'

'We had to settle for that ghastly sandwich place. The green one.'

'Subway? What's wrong with that?'

'All that greasy, microwaved meat? Terrible. I had to ask your father to find us a sofa in Costa instead. At least they have decent coffee. For a chain, anyway.'

'Hi, Dad.' Dan eyed the older man's lion-like sweep of white hair and lively brown eyes and held out his hand. His father took it and gave it a brief squeeze.

'You're just in time, my boy. I don't have it in me to fight off another group of tourists. Or keep your mother away from them.'

Maxine pursed her lips. 'You have no right to shoo away my fans. There's no harm in signing an autograph or two.'

'I prefer to drink my coffee in peace.'

'You're such a stick in the mud.'

'And you can't stand not being the centre of attention.'

As the pair began their customary bickering, Dan tuned it out and led his mother to the front passenger side. He held the door for her.

'See that, Julian, I raised him right. Such a good boy.' She pressed a dry, heavily perfumed kiss against his face and folded herself into the car.

Dan slammed the door behind her and scrubbed his cheek with his sleeve. 'Want a hand, Dad?'

Julian shook his head and climbed into the back seat. 'Let's just go.'

In the car, before Dan managed to fasten his seatbelt, the bickering started again.

'Let me buy you a new car, darling.' Maxine shoved one glossy fingernail into a hole in the dashboard. 'This thing is falling apart.'

He eased her hand away. 'It will, if you keep doing that. Besides, I like this car.'

'It isn't safe. I'll get you a BMW, or one of those sporty things my agent used to drive. You know the ones . . . a Lexus.'

'I don't want a new car.'

'It's no trouble. I know money must be tight what with that woman leeching it from your pockets.'

His pulse quickened. 'Leeching?'

Maxine patted her hair. It was already perfect, but she made a great show of curling it behind her ears before she spoke again. 'Carol, or whatever it is.'

'Karen.'

'Her. She's not working?'

'She's a student.'

'I knew she was too young for you.'

Dan curled and uncurled his toes within the confines of his shoes. He bit the inside of his cheek and counted to five before he spoke. 'She's thirty-one. It's a PhD.'

'That's a fancy way of saying she's living off the state, darling.'

'Steady, Maxine. Clearly the woman has some brains if she's doing something like that.' Julian leaned forward to pat Dan on the shoulder.

Dan opened his mouth to thank his father, but cut short when Maxine flapped a dismissive hand in his face. 'It's lazy, that's what it is. Those people who stay in education drinking and smoking, instead of working and contributing like everyone else. Lazy.'

'Like you?' Dan gritted his teeth.

'No, not like me. I'm retired, darling.'

'You haven't worked for twenty years.'

Maxine turned to face him. Her eyes, surrounded by delicate make-up, narrowed to thin slits. 'I've done my share. And I still contribute. I don't even draw my pension.'

'Only because you're not old enough.' Dan clutched the wheel harder than necessary and took a left at a sharp angle. 'What brings you all the way up here?'

A relieved sigh came from the back seat.

'It would be better if we got to your house first. I don't like to air my affairs in the street.'

Dan glanced around the interior of the car. 'I think you're safe, Mum.'

'I'd rather wait, thank you. I'll tell you over dinner.'

'You *are* staying, then?'

She pursed her lips. 'Don't say it like that. You make it sound as though Katherine hasn't prepared anything.'

'*Karen*, is a damn good cook, but even she needs more than half an hour to prepare a gluten-free, vegan meal for four.' He shot his mother an exasperated look.

'Oh.'

The single syllable lit a flame in Dan's belly. He exhaled to a slow count of ten. 'You didn't give us much warning. What were we supposed to do?'

'A resourceful woman always finds a way.'

Dan grunted. 'Tonight's my turn to cook.'

'You?' Maxine looked scandalised.

He looked her way. Her lips pursed and her nose wrinkled as if she'd smelled something horrid. Dan sighed loudly before he returned his attention to the road. 'I can cook.'

'Yes, of course, darling, but it's the least she can do. Or is she one of those awful feminist types who refuses to shave her underarms?'

'Mum please . . . I'll order a takeaway.'

'Fine, but no Chinese, or pizza and certainly no curry. I don't know what it is about you Leicester people. Everything has to be smothered in sauce and spices. Probably to hide the taste of dog and cat meat.'

Dan tightened his grip on the wheel and said nothing.

KAREN

Relief chased quickly by terror made Karen's skin flush first hot then cold. She straightened and turned her ear to listen a little better. Yes . . . jingling keys. The clunk of a key turning, followed by the squeal of laboured hinges as the front door opened.

'Hello?' a voice called.

'Dan?'

'Kaz? No, it's Pete.'

Karen sighed, relieved to put off the meet with Maxine a few more minutes. 'Thank God.' An instant later she remembered her naked body. The cage. She stiffened. A sour taste flooded her mouth. 'Shit. Peter?'

'Where are you?'

She hesitated then heard his footsteps pounding up the stairs.

The gritty truth of her entrapment finally broke through. There was no escape. Nowhere to hide. Her body was completely exposed.

Fuck . . .

'In the bedroom.' She closed her eyes. Her skin tingled, every muscle coiled tight with the urge to flee.

The door creaked open. Goosebumps trailed down her arms and legs.

A strangled whimper quivered through the air. 'Christ . . .'

Karen's eyes popped open.

Pete stood framed in the doorway. He wore faded blue jeans covered in old paint and a jacket with similar stains. A smudge of something black and oily smeared the side of his nose and his close-cropped hair glistened with sweat. His mouth hung open. 'How did you— what are you doing in there? Are you hurt?'

'Calm down for a second.'

'What the hell?' he whispered, voice broken and feeble.

'I'm okay—'

'But your arms.' He pointed, and his gaze followed his finger, across her arms and chest, lingering on her breasts before hiking back up to her shoulders. 'Are they bruises?'

'Whip marks.' She bit through each word, sharp and staccato like cracking bones.

'Fuck!'

'Pete, I'm fine. They'll be gone within an hour.'

'Jesus, Kaz.' His gaze skimmed the floor, pausing briefly on a black whip with a red handle. 'What's going on?'

After a few seconds of searching for an answer that wasn't embarrassing, Karen realised it didn't exist. She straightened her back and made her tone firm and clear while trying to ignore the way her breasts thrust forward every time she moved. 'We were playing.'

'Come again?'

'Playing,' she repeated, waggling her eyebrows.

He gave her a blank look.

'Oh, come on Pete, connect the dots. Playing? In the bedroom?'

Colour flooded his face: hot, healthy red. 'Oh.' He puffed out his cheeks. A grin blossomed on his lips. 'Kinky fuckers. You play with cages?'

Karen glared at the floor. She remembered her reluctance when Dan first suggested it and the sneaky way he eventually sweet-talked her into it. Damn his talented tongue.

'Not after this,' she muttered.

'Does he tie you up too? Have his wicked way?'

'It's not like that.'

Silence. When she looked up, Karen realised Pete hadn't stopped staring. His gaze traced her body, electric, like the crackling tip of a violet wand. Surprise mingled with the pleasure she felt at being looked at. Then guilt chased away both emotions.

'Eyes up, Pete.'

He snickered. 'Come on, Kaz. You look great.'

Her shoulders lifted. In his face, she saw sincere appreciation mingled with faint lust. Her legs trembled. 'Shut up.' The words lacked the venom she wanted. With effort she flicked the mental switch that controlled her voyeuristic side and jerked her head. 'The handcuff key is under the drawers. You need to free my hands.'

He stooped, groping beneath the unit with one hand. The whole time his gaze never left the cage. Aware of the view presented by the spreader bar, Karen swivelled round and gave him her back. 'Stop mucking around. It didn't go far.'

'You sure? I can't feel anything.'

'Try *looking*.'

She heard shuffling, thumps, and then the eventual slide of something hard moving across the carpet.

Pete touched her shoulder, skimming down her arm to her wrist. 'Christ, you're bendy.' His calloused fingers traced a path over her forearm.

She froze and bit her lip. *Does he have to touch me like that?* The cuffs clicked and both bracelets slid away. Without turning back, she reached for the buckles around her ankles. 'Thanks, now give me that blanket. The one in the corner.'

Closing her legs immediately lessened the ache in her hips, and when Pete pushed the fuzzy blanket between the bars, it took great effort not to snatch it. She wrapped it around her body, took a deep breath, then swivelled back round. With great care, she tucked the edges in around her thighs and arse, covering every scrap of skin from the neck down.

'Dan said you needed help. He didn't tell me what was going on or else I'd have come prepared.' He smirked.

She gaped. His expression matched those she saw on men shamelessly stalking the 'career girls' loitering in backstreets or dark alleys near the train station.

To see that look directed at her; to feel the heat of his gaze sliding over her naked skin, knotted her stomach and made bile rise in her throat.

Pete's smirk vanished. 'Don't look at me like that, I'm kidding.' He shifted beneath her stare and finally dropped his gaze. 'What am I supposed to be doing?'

'Dan lost the cage key.' She scanned the floor. 'You've got to get me out before he comes back with his parents.'

That brought his gaze up pretty damn quick. He whistled through his teeth. 'Why the hell is he bringing them here?'

'Surprise visit.'

'Wow. You two are just— how can you—'

'Pete.' She slapped the bars. 'Did you hear me? Find the key.'

'Yeah, yeah, yeah.'

He began to search.

Pete laid a bra wire, two pound coins and a tube of lube on the bookcase. Then he cleared the floor, stacking the whip, a flogger, and a purple dildo on the chest of drawers. With each new toy, his features tightened. A blush spread across his jaw and down his neck. When he picked up a large Perspex butt plug and held it up to the light, she flinched and closed her eyes. She reopened them to find him staring at a brown plastic box attached to a plug. The long shaft had a glass attachment with a bell-shaped end.

He licked his lips. 'What the hell is this thing?'

'A violet wand,' she whispered.

'A what? No, don't tell me.' His hands shook as he laid it on the bed. 'Sorry, Kaz, it ain't here.'

A glance at the wall clock made Karen's stomach clench. 'They'll be back soon. Maxine can't see me like this.' Even under the blanket she began to shiver. 'Do something.'

'I'm not bloody Houdini.'

'But you *are* a builder. Don't you have something to fix this? Like a tool?'

'I didn't bring the van.'

She looked at his paint splattered clothes.

He followed her gaze. 'Painting doesn't need screwdrivers and hammers, Kaz. And a paintbrush ain't going to help you.'

'Please, Pete.' She clutched her hair, aware that her hands were shaking. A flutter in her stomach made her wince. 'You don't get it, Maxine is just— what am I going to do?'

'Breathe, Kaz.'

'I *am* breathing.'

'Don't bite my head off. How the hell did you lose the key, anyway?'

'Ask Dan,' she snapped, mulling on the memory of him playfully dangling the key over his open mouth.

'Well, I'm trying to help. A little gratitude would be nice.'

She sighed. 'Sorry.'

'It's okay. Just let me think.' He paced around the cage.

'Can you use something in here to bend the bars? Maybe I can squeeze out.'

'No. It's reinforced steel. But these corners have screws in them and the door too. Where are Dan's tools?'

'No idea.'

He stared.

'I don't live here.' She spread her hands. 'How would I know?'

'You're not making this easy.'

'Oh, excuse me. Maybe next time I'll keep a handy tool box under the bed.'

'That's probably not a bad idea.' Pete ran his fingers through his hair. 'Okay. Be right back.'

Abandoned again.

Karen snuggled deeper into the fluffy embrace of the blanket and took several deep breaths. She watched the clock, trying not to mentally chart Dan's journey to and from the train station. Three minutes later Pete returned to the room with a handful of knives.

'One of these should do it,' he said.

Karen watched him work. Several discarded knives later he found one that suited him and started twisting. Soon, the sound of grinding metal chased away the soft hiss of his breathing. His fingers shook as he worked.

'Pete?'

'What? Ow! Fuck!' Pete reared up with his index finger gripped in his fist. Blood welled through the gap in his fingers.

'Are you okay?'

'Aside from slicing my finger open?'

'Sorry.' She glanced at the clock again.

'What's wrong?'

'How long is this going to take?'

'Ages using this piece of crap.' He dropped the bloodied knife. 'I need a proper screwdriver. You must know where he keeps stuff like that.'

She shook her head.

'I'll phone him, then.'

'No.' Karen pressed against the cage, clutching her blanket as the imagined conversation played through her mind. 'You can't phone him.'

'Why?'

'He'll be with his parents by now. How will he explain that?'

'Fuck, Kaz, what do you want from me?'

She pressed her fingertips to her temples, staring at Pete and the blood dripping down his hairy forearm, off the end of his elbow. A tiny pool formed on the carpet.

'Try the kitchen drawers. He fixed a shelf last week; maybe he left some stuff out.'

'Progress.'

'Are you sure you're okay?' Her question chased his retreating back as he headed for the kitchen.

The blanket scratched her bare skin and the silence of the room pressed in, more claustrophobic than the bars of the cage. She longed to pace and drummed her fingers against her thigh in poor substitute. Nervous energy flooded her limbs, making her jiggle first one leg then the other. She gnawed on her fingernails and returned to watching the clock.

Then the front door open a second time and Dan's cheery voice floated up the stairs. 'Hey babe, I'm home!'

DAN

Dan stepped into the house. His pulse filled the back of his throat.

He checked the sitting room, found it empty, and knew Karen was still trapped upstairs. 'Shit.' His shoulders slumped. 'Tea, Mum?'

Maxine stepped over the threshold and into the hallway, frowning at a framed picture of the Manchester United team of 1998. 'Yes, darling, that would be lovely. Thank you.'

He pointed. 'Sit in the front room; I'll bring it.'

'Wonderful. Come Julian.' Without pausing, Maxine marched into the sitting room. Julian followed, shaking his head and rubbing his eyelids with the tips of his fingers.

Pausing only long enough to see them sit, Dan darted into the kitchen. There he found Pete, riffling through drawers and wearing an expression like he'd sucked a lemon.

'Hey Pete, is she out?' He lowered his voice, conscious of the short distance between himself and the sitting room.

His friend whirled around and dropped a knife onto the floor. His upper lip curled, showing off a glint of gold in the top row of teeth. 'Bastard,' he snarled.

Dan flinched away from the unexpected show of venom. 'I know—'

'Do you?'

'I'm sorry.' His gaze strayed to the knife and the small trail of blood drops across the floor. 'What happened to you?'

Pete blinked, as if noticing the red stains for the first time. 'The knife slipped.'

'Is she out?'

'No, genius. What were you thinking? Why didn't you warn me?'

'No time.'

'No time to warn me she was naked?' Pete scrubbed his hands through his short scruffy hair. 'You could have covered her up.'

The simplicity of it made Dan cringe. Perhaps he'd overreacted. A reoccurring problem where his mother was concerned. Rather than voicing his doubts, he crossed his arms and tilted his chin. 'You don't understand.'

'Clearly not.' Again, the edge in Pete's voice cut the air like a bare razor blade. 'I need a screwdriver.'

'In the shed, on the floor, near the paint brushes.'

'Thanks.' Pete stomped out the back door, leaving a small trail of blood.

Dan followed and had almost reached the door when Julian entered behind him.

'Your mother's fretting over this tea. You got mint or fennel?'

'No.'

'Son . . .'

'I didn't know you were coming. She can have Earl Grey and be happy with it.' Dan saw the startled look in his father's eyes and took a deep breath. In a softer voice he added, 'Do you want one?'

'Coffee, boy, you know me.'

Dan filled the kettle and grabbed three mugs. 'Is she still in the living room?'

'No, she went upstairs.'

His stomach dropped so fast it threatened to hit his toes. 'What?'

'She wanted to use the bathroom. What's wrong?'

Dan fumbled the mugs onto the counter and ran for the stairs, climbing them two at a time. Halfway up he twisted his ankle and limped up the remainder. He rounded the corner on the landing in time to catch his mother with her hand on the door to the master bedroom.

'Mum, wait!'

'Hi, darling.' She beamed at him. 'Just having a look around. Love the new wallpaper. Does it go all the way through?'

'Don't go in there.' He approached with his hands extended, waving as if directing traffic.

'Why?'

Dan chewed his bottom lip. 'It's not fit for guests.'

'Silly boy, I don't mind a little mess.'

'I'm embarrassed.' He knocked her hand away from the handle. 'I'd rather you didn't see it.'

She crossed her arms and arched an eyebrow.

'You raised me better than that. I don't want you to see what a slob I am.'

'But the wallpaper—'

'Is exactly the same. I'll show you later, once I've tidied up.'

'You know, Daniel.' She pursed her lips. 'If that woman of yours was worth anything, she'd tidy up.'

Dan heard a sharp exclamation from beyond the door.

Maxine stiffened. 'What was that?'

'What?' He widened his eyes.

'That noise?'

'I didn't hear anything. Just come downstairs and have your tea.'

Maxine reached around him. 'I really don't mind the mess. Let me see.'

'No.' Again he shoved her hand aside.

'Daniel, that hurt.'

'Sorry, but please, let me tidy up first. Then you can see.' He held out his hand, adopting the voice he remembered using to recite his most successful Christmas wish lists. 'Let's go downstairs. Have you used the bathroom already?'

'Yes, and I can't believe you're using that thin, cheap paper. Why not use soft rolls? Like the ones we use?'

He fought the urge to roll his eyes. Nit-picking and thinly veiled disapproval were expressions of motherly love he could do without.

Instead, he took her by the hand and coaxed her toward the stairs. 'You're right. Remind me which ones you use so I can buy some next time.'

'I will. And be sure you do.' She sniffed. 'While I know that girl must be a financial drain you can at least buy decent toilet paper.'

With his shoulders hunched against the sound of another indignant squeak beyond the door, Dan marched down the stairs. He held his mother's hand all the way into the kitchen where clouds of steam told him the kettle had boiled.

Julian stood near the sink, pouring water into mugs. 'Sugar?'

'No, thank you.' Maxine waved her hand.

'I meant Daniel.'

'And I said "no", Julian. He's getting chubby. Probably too many takeaways.'

Dan cringed away from the fingers jabbing his rib cage. *Just can't help it, can you, Mum? What next, my hair?*

Julian blew through his moustache. 'How do you want this tea, my boy?'

'Two sugars please.' Dan ignored the sigh of disapproval from his mother and steered her into a chair.

'Your friend is outside, by the way.' Julian pointed to the window. 'In your shed.'

Maxine craned her neck. 'Has he been here all this time?'

'Yes.' Dan rubbed his foot over the trail of blood on the floor tiles. 'He's helping me in the bedroom. You know he's a builder.'

'And you left him here alone with Kate?'

'Karen.'

She smoothed her skirt. 'Karen then. Was that wise?'

'Why wouldn't it be?'

'You know better than I do, but— no. Don't mind me. I'm sure it's nothing.'

He stared at her, his entire body tingling with the effort it took not to take the bait. It was too much. 'What is it, Mum?'

'Well, where is she?'

'Upstairs.'

'Getting dressed?'

'Maybe. What are you getting at?'

'Nothing. Though . . .' Maxine glanced out the window. 'Your friend is a bit scruffy, isn't he? Dishevelled?'

'So?'

More skirt smoothing. 'Perhaps he dressed in a hurry?'

'Tea, Maxine.'

Dan closed his mouth over his reply, grateful for his father's timely interruption. He used the gap to flex his fingers. 'Pete helped me do the wallpaper. That's all. He's probably clearing tools from the bedroom.' He gave his mother a significant glance.

'He won't let me see the master room, Julian.'

'And why should he? He's not a child.'

Though their relationship had never been physical, in that moment Dan could have kissed his father. He settled for smiling.

'Does that mean I shouldn't see his lovely new wallpaper?'

Content that his parents had returned to bickering, Dan rushed into the garden. He reached Pete just as he held up a screwdriver.

'Near the paintbrushes, my hairy arse.'

Dan tangled his hands in his hair. 'I'm under a bit of pressure right now.'

'Whatever. Let's sort out this bloody cage.'

'Please hurry.'

'Yeah, yeah, yeah.' Pete trudged inside.

Dan followed and positioned his chair to block the way out. He noticed a fresh trail of blood across the floor tiles and glanced at his mother who was scrubbing at the tabletop with a sponge. 'Your tea is getting cold.'

She moved to the counter beside the sink and kept wiping. 'Does she ever clean?'

'Mum, please.'

'I'm just asking.'

'This is *my* house,' he snapped, patience beaten so thin he could poke holes through it. 'When I can be bothered, I clean. I cook. Karen spends her time here *with* me, not clucking like a mother hen.'

'She's here often?'

'Every day.'

'Oh.' Maxine stopped cleaning long enough to wrinkle her nose. 'What's her house like?'

'She shares a flat with a friend.'

'A flat? Oh dear.'

'You used to live in one.'

'Before I got my break on *Home with Mr. Barclay.*' Her chin tilted as she said it. 'Then I moved straight into a nice clean semi. Caroline's old enough to own her own place. Why share?'

Dan turned his gaze skyward and whispered Karen's name in his head as if to secure his own memory of it. 'Does it matter?'

'I'm curious.'

'She had to finance the PhD herself. Rent is cheaper than a mortgage.' As Dan lied, he realised he had no idea why Karen still shared with Cindy. But he did know the idea of discussing Karen's living arrangements made him want to crawl into a deep hole and never climb out.

'That's something. But is she moving in with you?'

He hesitated, weighing out the projected satisfaction of lying against the ease of telling the truth. He opted for the latter. 'We don't have any plans for that.'

The smug, knowing smile on Maxine's lips made him want to change his answer.

'Here, my boy,' Julian nudged his shoulder with a steaming mug.

Dan took it and gratefully slurped from the rim.

'Darling, have you fixed the garden yet?'

'Give him a break, woman.' Julian actually raised his voice, a rare and frightening occurrence. Even Maxine glanced at him askance.

'A simple question. What's the matter with you two today?'

Dan rubbed his forehead. 'I wanted to do the house first. The garden can wait.'

'Do you still have that ghastly pond?'

'I filled it in.'

'Good. May I at least see that?'

Sighing, Dan put his tea down and reopened the back door. He ushered his mother through then followed. Julian joined them.

Maxine marched to the bottom of the garden and stopped at the edge of a patch of freshly turned earth. 'Even without flowers it's much nicer like this.'

Dan shrugged.

'And now you have space for a vegetable patch. Organic food is good for you.'

'Mum . . .'

'I read an article last week about all the chemicals in our food. Terrible. It's a wonder any of us are still alive.'

He nodded.

'I forgot my tea. One moment, darling.' Maxine pranced back to the house.

Dan put his head in his hands. He gave a wordless groan.

Julian patted his back. 'Deep breaths, my boy.'

'Why can't she just be normal?'

The older man smiled. 'You never did understand, that is normal. For your mother.'

'Every time she speaks, I feel like I'm going through a wrangler.'

'Try living with her.' He grinned. 'It does look better, by the way. The pond was too much work for a busy man like you. And you don't need a veggie garden.'

'I only said it to shut her up.'

'I thought so. As if you have time with this girlfriend of yours.'

'Don't you start, too.'

Julian's eyes twinkled. 'What? I think she's lovely; intelligent clearly, dedicated obviously. It sounds like you struck gold.'

Dan gave his first real smile in hours. 'Thanks, Dad. Convince Mum, will you?'

'I'll try. Where is she?'

'Tea, she said.'

'What's taking so long?'

Dan looked at the house. He frowned and peered through the window into the empty kitchen. Cold knots filled his stomach. He closed his eyes. 'She's not there. I think she's in my bedroom.'

KAREN

Karen clutched the bars of the cage. The blanket slipped off her shoulders but she made no move to pull it up, staring instead at the closed door while her knuckles paled. Beyond it, she heard Dan beg his mother to join him downstairs, diverting her with some nonsense about toilet paper.

'Be sure that you do,' Maxine's high, nasal tones floated through the door. 'While I know that girl must be a financial drain you can at least buy decent toilet paper.'

Karen slammed her fist against the cage bars. 'Screw you, Maxine.'

Their footsteps retreated on the stairs. She had no idea what Dan's response might have been, but she knew enough not to hope for much.

'Bitch.'

Again she hit and kicked the cage bars. Silence followed broken only by the thunderous pound of blood in her ears. She sank back on to her knees and stared at the door, half sorry that the chance to vent her frustrations had been snatched away by Dan's timely intervention. She leaned back and kicked the bars again, over and over, each kick timed to land in concert with her grunts of fury. The noisy assault continued until Pete returned holding a screwdriver. 'Hey, calm down.'

She kicked the cage again. 'Are you serious?'

'They'll hear you.'

'I could give a shit. Did you hear her? Bitch! She's worse than before. I hate her so much.'

'I know, but—'

'You know how it feels to have someone look down on you because you don't fit their idea of what's good enough?'

'No, but—'

'No. So shut up and get me out of here.'

Pete gazed at his shoes. 'I found a screwdriver.' When she didn't answer, he set to work. He released all the screws on the first hinge, despite his injured finger, then began the next. Eventually the front panel clanged forward and dangled from its bolt and padlock.

Karen grinned and eased through the gap. 'Thank God.' Her spine creaked as she straightened it and lifted her arms above her head for the first time in hours.

'You're welcome.' He tossed the screwdriver onto the bed.

'Sorry, Pete. I didn't mean to snap. Rough day. You did great.' Her smile faded when she followed his gaze down her naked frame. She snagged the blanket from within the cage and wrapped it tight around her once more. 'You can go now.'

He turned to the door and looked back. Though he refused to meet her gaze the crimson flush to his cheeks was easy to see. 'This "playing" you do . . . does it involve friends?'

'Get out!' she shrieked.

He fled.

Karen considered the merits of hiding beneath the bed and never coming out, but the thought of Maxine's smug smile and haughty stare convinced her not to. Instead she snatched up the screwdriver and attacked the other sides of the cage. Pete made the job look easy, but sweat soon beaded on her back and forehead. More than once the tool slipped on the reluctant screws and only sharp reflexes saved her fingers from similar damage.

Several minutes later, the cage lay in six pieces that she stacked and shoved under the bed. The door creaked open just as she smoothed the duvet back into place.

'Oh, you *are* here.' The snide inflection in that posh voice made her gut clench.

She whirled round. Glared. 'Maxine.'

'Nice to see you, Carol.'

'Karen.' Her molars gnashed together.

'Of course.' Maxine shoved the door open and entered the room. She spared Karen only a glance before inspecting the walls and carpet. 'It looks very nice. He could have had more colour though.'

'We like blue.'

'We?' Surprise temporarily broke through Maxine's veneer of disdain. 'This is Daniel's house.'

Karen hesitated, tugging the edges of the blanket. Yes, it was Dan's house, despite all the time they spent together in it. She tucked the corners of the blanket beneath her armpits and tilted her chin. 'He asked me to help. We decided together.'

'Does that happen often?'

'Yes,' she said, earlier hesitation vanished. The unhappy twist to Maxine's mouth gave her an absurd rush of pleasure. 'Is that all? I need to get dressed.'

'You keep clothes here?'

'Of course.' Another wicked spike of pleasure surged through Karen when she saw the tightening of Maxine's lips. 'I wake here most mornings so I keep some in those drawers.'

Maxine sniffed, as if something unpleasant had crawled up her nose. 'Daniel does enjoy company.' She arched an eyebrow. 'Last week he told me about a pretty woman he met at work. Sandra. I think he really likes her.' Though coy in her body language, the nonchalance of her tone didn't fit the grim smile on her face.

'Yes, I know Sandra, she's lovely. So's her girlfriend.'

'Girlfriend?' Maxine's voice rose several octaves. Her eyebrows shot up her forehead to hide beneath her fringe.

'He didn't tell you she's gay? And married?' Karen didn't bother hiding her smirk. 'Must have slipped his mind.'

With visible effort, Maxine gathered herself for the next attack. Karen waited with her tongue wedged between her teeth.

'Sorry to disturb your day in bed. Sleeping off last night's drunken revelry?'

Karen opened her mouth then snapped it shut again. No matter how she felt, she knew that to blurt out the truth would only make matters worse. Even her own, liberal parents knew nothing of her unconventional relationship with the man eleven years her senior.

She settled for a half-truth. 'Dan and I were in bed when you called. I thought I'd take advantage of the half hour catnap. I know he would have preferred to rest too, but he's a charitable guy.' She turned to the dresser to hide her triumphant smile.

Pounding footsteps advanced up the stairs. Dan burst into the room. 'I can explain!' he cried. A pause. 'Oh.'

'Explain what, darling?'

Karen glanced over her shoulder, enjoying the flicker of confusion in Dan's eyes. *That's right,* she mused. *Sweat it out, you bastard.*

'Nothing.' He scratched the back of his neck. 'I mean, your tea is getting cold, Mum.'

'Oh, I completely forgot it, silly me.'

'Don't worry, Maxine, the occasional senior moment is nothing to worry about.'

Dan gaped and slumped against the doorframe, hiding his face in his hands.

Karen ignored him and grinned at Maxine. 'Do you need a hand down the stairs? If you don't mind waiting I'll come with you.'

'I'm fine.' Maxine tossed her head, gave one last glare, and stalked out.

Karen narrowed her eyes and watched Dan listen to her retreating steps. As soon as they were gone she unleashed her anger. 'If you ever do that to me again—'

'Did you have to be so mean?'

'Mean?' A gasp caught in her throat. She stared at him. '*Me,* mean? You didn't hear her earlier. Dan, she's vile.'

'She's my mother.'

'And *I'm* your slave. Doesn't that count for anything?'

He glanced over his shoulder. 'Keep your voice down.'

'No.' Karen sliced the air with her palm. Her blanket fell to the floor. Goosebumps raced across her skin, but fury chased the cold away. 'You left me in that cage not knowing if Pete would come. You left me naked. You left me *hoping* that

Pete would show up without telling him what to expect. How do you think that made me feel?'

'Probably great. You love being watched.'

'Not by your best friend! You should have seen the look he gave me.' The memory of it made her shudder. 'I was a piece of meat he wanted to fuck.'

Dan shut the door behind him. 'You're exaggerating.'

'Am I? Dan, please understand, when we do this, I do it for *you*. I'm caged and serving you, but you didn't check with me, you didn't give me a choice. There was no safe word. We weren't in scene.' She rubbed her arms. Her skin prickled with the memory of Pete's gaze on her body. 'It was just me, naked in a cage and he looked at me like I was a star from Channel XXX. I'll never be able to look at him again.'

'It's not that bad.'

'How would you know? Have you been locked up in any cages in front of my sex-starved friends, recently?'

He pressed his lips together. A flicker of sadness passed through his eyes, but it vanished so quickly Karen convinced herself that she'd made it up. His hand stretched out.

She stumbled back. 'Don't. Please. You can't touch me right now.'

The hand dropped out of range 'I panicked.' His voice trembled. 'I couldn't think. Mum was coming and I just didn't want— I'm sorry you had to go through that.'

'Good.'

'Will you come down now?'

She imagined Maxine downstairs, making herself comfortable on the sofa suite picked in Karen's favourite colours, sipping tea Karen chose. She jerked her head. 'No chance.'

'But they came to see us.'

Karen returned to pulling drawers open. 'They came to see *you*. And I'm not speaking to that woman until you at least admit what she's doing.'

'She's not doing anything.'

She bunched her hands into fists as that familiar urge to scream returned. How could he say that? How could he not see?

He stood so close, that unruly tumble of hair dangling into his face again. He jerked it away with a toss of his head, a gesture so familiar that her resolve almost softened. He always did that, right before spanking her or ordering her to her knees. Karen watched his eyes, waiting for him to recognise how ridiculous he sounded, but he didn't. He never did— not where Maxine was concerned.

'I'm staying here.' She turned away to hide her face.

While tugging on a red bra and knickers, Karen felt Dan's eyes on her back. She ignored him, pulling a vest from a lower drawer and squirming into it. By the time she'd found a pair of comfortable jogging bottoms, Dan had left, his exit marked by a gentle click from the door.

She sighed and slumped onto the bed to bury her face against the pillows.

DAN

Back in the kitchen, Dan lowered his forehead to rest on the table. Behind, his mother buzzed around like an oversized bee on speed. She washed mugs and wiped surfaces, while humming "Peggy Sue" slightly out of key. She slammed four glass tumblers into the cupboard.

Dan cringed. 'Mum?'

'Yes, darling?'

'Are you okay?'

'Of course. Why?' She shoved another mug into the cupboard.

'You seem tense.'

'I'm fine.'

Dan gritted his teeth. 'Bullshit.'

'Daniel!'

'Then talk to me. And stop cracking my dishes.'

Maxine paused. An expectant hush whispered through the room. Even Julian looked up, eyes wide beneath his bushy eyebrows.

'Really, darling, I'm just tired from the trip.'

Unclenching his fists, Dan made himself nod. He even managed a half smile. 'What did you want to tell me?'

She gave him a blank look.

'You had something to tell me in the car. You said you'd tell me over dinner.'

'Did I?'

Yes! You did, you crazy woman. You made me stick another fork in my relationship just so you didn't have to take a cab. He blew a harsh breath through his nose and focused on the fact he loved her, despite how difficult she made it.

'Yes, and it had to be pretty important to bring you here from Ely on public transport.'

'I don't know what you mean. I just wanted to visit my favourite boy.'

'Your *only* boy.'

Maxine flicked a dishcloth at his face in what she probably thought was a playful manner. 'That's right and you haven't given me a proper hug yet.'

Dan slouched forward.

She yanked him into her and crushed his face against her perfumed throat. She smoothed back his hair and kissed his cheek. When she licked her thumb and aimed for his forehead, he jerked back.

'I'm not a child.'

'You'll always be my baby.'

'Leave the boy alone, Maxine,' said Julian. 'And sit down, you're making me dizzy.'

'But it's so untidy.'

Dan escaped his mother's octopus arms and leaned against the fridge. 'You don't have to do this, Mum.'

Rather than answering, Maxine put away a stack of plates, cleaned the top of the stove, and filled the kettle. 'I wouldn't have to if Caroline was doing her job.'

'*Karen*, Mum. Her name is Karen! And she doesn't have to clean my house.'

'She should do her share, darling. You can't keep her for nothing while she does this PhD or whatever it is.'

Dan rubbed his eyes. 'I'm not doing this. Not now.'

'I'm just saying.' Maxine spread her hands and widened her eyes. 'If she's going to stay here, eat your food, use your utilities, and spend time alone with your male friends, the least she can do is clean up. I mean look at this; is that blood on the floor?'

'Mum,' he snapped, trying to head off the inevitable follow up question of where it came from.

'Fine.' She sat down, crossed her legs and placed her hands on her raised knee. 'I bet Darla never gives her mother so much trouble.'

'Who?'

'Darla Shields. Your friend from school.'

Dan stretched his mind back. 'The chubby kid who smeared mud in my hair?'

Maxine beamed. 'I knew you'd remember. You were so close.'

'We were five. She put frog spawn down the back of my shirt.'

Darla Shields had also poured glue into his lunch box, tried to cut his hair with safety scissors, and pushed him into the fish pond when nobody was looking. Just thinking her name conjured the memory of slimy fingers of algae wrapped about his face while filthy water filled his mouth.

The kettle boiled and a cloud of steam puffed out. Julian slid away to make more drinks.

Dan narrowed his eyes. 'Why bring up Darla?'

'What?' Said Maxine with unconvincing innocence. She often used the same voice when discussing "his future." A future that, as far as she was concerned, should include babies, marriage, and a better job.

'It's been thirty years since I last saw her. What does she have to do with anything?'

A dark glint flickered in Maxine's eyes. 'I wasn't going to say anything, but since you bring her up—'

'Me?'

'She's moving here soon. Vanessa told me.'

'Who?'

'Darla's mother. She's been part of my quilting group for years. Anyway, Vanessa said Darla would be moving to this area next week, but she doesn't know anybody. I told her you'd be happy to take her out.'

'Excuse me?'

'Yes, you can try the pub up the street. Maybe the movies. I'm sure you'll have a lovely night.'

As if on cue, a thump from upstairs reminded him of Karen. He thought of her face, her smile as she gave every part of herself to him. Next to the memory of Darla's triumphant sneer as he shivered beneath a lily pad, he needed little help to make up his mind.

'Are you serious?' he stammered. 'I can't do that.'

'Why not?'

'Dad,' he begged, a desperate bid for aid from the only man his mother might actually heed. 'Help me out here.'

Julian held out a fresh mug of tea. When no one took it, he helped himself to a sip and said nothing.

'I don't understand what the problem is, darling.'

Dan surged to his feet. His chair clattered to the floor. 'I have a girlfriend!'

'Karen?' A sneer tugged the corner of Maxine's mouth. 'You clearly don't see a future with her, so why bother?'

'Now what are you talking about?'

'At this stage of your last relationship, you were living together. Do you remember Bethany?'

Dan reeled as though punched. He tried to sit then remembered his chair was on the floor. It took several tries to retrieve it with his fingers shaking so badly. When he finally managed to right the chair, he eased into it while staring at the floor. 'I remember. Clearly better than you.'

'Now there was a nice girl. Polite. Respectful. How could you let her get away?'

His fists clutched to form white nubs on the table. 'Mum, do you actually remember her?'

'Of course. She made beautiful dinners, kept your old place spotless . . .'

Yes, kept the flat spotless, hacked into my email account, read my text messages, opened my mail . . .

Licking his lips didn't help chase away the bitter taste in Dan's mouth. He swallowed, but the uncomfortable itch at the back of his throat refused to leave. 'We drifted apart.'

'Why? You were perfect for each other.'

'No, we weren't.' Dan pounded his fist on the table. From the corner of his eye he saw Julian jump and slop tea over his hands.

'Son?'

'I'm fine, Dad. Sorry.'

'I understand.'

Dan sighed. Of all the things his father probably did understand, his relationship with Bethany wasn't one of them.

'Poor thing,' Maxine cooed. 'You still miss her, don't you?'

Pete chose that moment to put his head around the door. He had red stains on his shirt and a plaster wrapped clumsily around one finger. He swept his gaze over the gathering. 'Sorry, I'll just go.'

'No, wait a second.' Dan waved him back. 'I need to talk to you. Wait for me in the living room?'

Pete's expression flattened. 'Sure.'

Maxine watched him go. 'What an odd man.'

'Mum.' Dan looked back at her. 'Is that what this was about? To fix me up with a girl from nursery school?'

She smoothed her skirt and hair though neither required it. 'I came to help you, darling. As any mother would.'

'I don't need help.' Dan's pulse quickened as he finally understood what he needed do. Tugging his phone from his pocket, he swiped the screen for his saved numbers.

'What are you doing?'

'Calling you a cab,' he muttered, taking time to savour the look of shock on his mother's face. 'You can wait outside.'

Dan lowered himself to the sofa and buried his head in his hands. He dragged his fingers over his face until the skin pulled. Across from him, legs crossed at the ankle, Pete popped the lid off a bottle of Budweiser and passed it over. 'Here, mate.'

Two large swallows later, Dan felt calmer. 'What is it about parents?' he whispered. 'Are they all insane?'

'Mine are.'

'Where's Karen?'

Pete stared at his shoes.

His stomach knotted. 'She's still pissed off? How many more times can I apologise?'

'Women, right?'

'Right.' Dan took another swig. 'I'm really sorry about this.'

A smile played around Pete's lips. 'Free boobs. It was brilliant.'

'It's not. It's a mess.'

'If you say so.'

'You don't think it's a steaming pile of shit? She'll never talk to me again.'

'But if you can still put her in that cage what's the problem?' He gulped his own drink and sat back. His smile widened, but something in his eyes didn't match.

'Fuck you, Pete,' he snarled. The events of the day finally snipped through the last of his patience. 'That's my girlfriend.'

'Yeah?'

'Of course she is. What do you think is happening here?'

'I have no idea, but it looks like some rough, kinky shit.'

'You could call it that.'

Pete took a deep breath. He sat forward and directed his words at the floor between his feet. 'Did you hurt her?'

Dan became very still. His breathing lowered, but the rush of his blood in his ears became a roar. 'Excuse me?'

'She had big red marks all over her arms, shoulder and back. She said they'd fade.'

'They will.' His voice emerged far more defensive than he intended but Dan couldn't help it. He glanced left and right, then at his friend. 'They will fade.'

'So you *did* hit her?'

He flinched. The words struck him like a punch. He felt sick inside, shaky and hot. 'I didn't hurt her.'

'You hit her. What the hell is wrong with you?'

'Nothing. We were playing and—' He licked his lips.

He doesn't believe me. Why doesn't he believe me? I wouldn't— I would never.

His grip tightened around his bottle. Sweat slipped down his jaw and into the collar of his shirt. 'I didn't hurt her, Pete.'

'That's what she said, but that's what women say when they're scared.' His gaze intensified.

'She's not scared.' He bit off each word, grinding his teeth so hard the tension sprawled across his skull as a full–blown headache. 'Christ, you think I'm actually hurting her? Beating her up?'

'You are.'

'I'm not!' His shout filled the room and bounced off the walls. He heard the echo, but it was in his head, a thunderous loop over and over in the cavern of his mind. *I wouldn't hurt her. Not Karen. Never— not after— I wouldn't hurt her. Not for real.*

'You hit her.'

'In scene,' he insisted desperately. 'It's part of the fun— the game.'

'Beating Karen is a game to you?'

Dan jumped to his feet. In that moment he imagined punching his friend. Grinding his fist into that steady, accusing expression to wipe it away. 'You're twisting my words.'

'You're telling me that you beat your girlfriend. What's to twist? I sat here thinking about it while you talked to your folks. The more I thought about it, the more scared I got. Twice I nearly called the police, but I wanted to let you explain yourself first. You're my friend, Dan, but this is fucked up.'

'Don't do that. Don't assume you understand what's going on. I wouldn't hurt her. Not for real. I'm not that person.' His words tumbled over each other in his desperation to get them out. Panic threatened to take over but he held it at bay. Just. If only he could make Pete understand.

'What else should I assume? You phone me saying "get over quick and help Karen."' When Pete looked up something fierce burned in his narrowed grey eyes. 'I tear over here like a fucking getaway driver and find Karen in a cage with a bunch of weird torture tools.'

'They're not torture tools.'

'Yeah? Because those marks looked nasty.'

'I didn't break the skin. I never do.'

'You've done that before?' Pete's mouth dropped open. He stood. 'I'm taking her out of here. Now. Tonight. Don't try to stop me.'

'What's wrong with you? Listen to yourself. You know me. We've been friends for years. You *know* me. I'm not that guy.'

As Pete marched towards the sitting room door, Dan ran to block his path. 'Just wait and listen.' He begged his friend. 'Please, you owe me that much.'

'I don't owe you anything except a good slap with that bottle.'

Not once breaking eye contact, Dan bent to rest his Budweiser on the floor. He straightened slowly, with his arms held out palm up. Everything trembled, from his knees to his elbows, but those tremors were nothing compared to the cold seeping into his bones. It chilled him from the inside out until he could barely speak. But he had to. There was no choice left.

'I know you watch fetish porn,' Dan whispered. 'The harder stuff. Don't bother denying it, I've seen your computer. I know you understand when I say we were in the middle of a scene. Dominant and submissive. BDSM.'

'None of the stuff I watch has marks like that.'

'Your stuff is tame. But it's all there. Log into any fetish site you like. Watch the interviews. Watch the sick bastards like me cracking whips over their screaming women. Watch them get off on the tears.' He looked away, suddenly sickened by his own wants and needs.

Pete's jaw dropped. He took a step back. 'You're serious, aren't you?' The fury leeched from his eyes and left behind a faint echo, overlain with confusion. 'BDSM?'

Dan risked lowering his arms but he still didn't look at Pete. 'Now you know. Karen's my girlfriend, but she's my submissive too. She's my slave.'

Pete paled. 'You have a sex slave? Did you buy her over from Saint Lucia or something? What the hell does that even mean? People go to prison for that shit.'

'Pete! For fuck's sake, listen to me. Karen's my girlfriend. She's just like any other girlfriend, but there's another layer, a master/slave element that we add in the bedroom. And sometimes outside the bedroom too.'

'There's a word for people like you.'

Dan cringed. The phrase too closely resembled one he'd heard at his first and last Munch.

In a busy pub in the middle of Leicester one cold Sunday lunchtime, he dared to meet with other men and women who enjoyed "a bit of kink." As he sipped lemonade, nibbled homemade cupcakes, and listened to stories of play parties and fetish fairs, he saw a faint glimmer of what it could be like to socialise with those who felt as he did.

The quiet group of ten "kinksters" made him instantly welcome in a way few other social gatherings had. No pushy questions or battles of ego, just quiet acceptance. He met men and women who craved control. Who needed it, in varying degrees, to feel whole in themselves. He met others who longed to give up that control, in part or in full, to someone they trusted to respect and care for them.

Toward the end of the meet, a man slouched past their group of tables. Despite the early hour he was clearly drunk, swaying to and fro, and spilling the contents of his pint glass.

'Are you from that bunch of fetish freaks?' he asked, leaning low to peer over the table. 'Those weird fuckers too sad to get real dates?'

Jolted from his memories by a cough from Pete, Dan tilted his chin and looked him in the eye. 'There are several words for "people like me,"' he whispered. 'Us and everybody else with a kink. Sick. Unhinged. Disgusting. Sinful.'

Pete looked away. Dan grabbed his grubby shirt and shook it. 'Look at me!' He saw the startled look in his friend's eyes, but he didn't care. This was too important. 'Are those the words you meant, Pete? I've got more. How about "a giant clusterfuck of broken, socially malfunctioning deviants"? I always liked that one.'

'I'm sorry—'

'Karen and I have an open, honest relationship, which is more than I can say for a bunch of vanilla couples out there.' He lowered his voice, staring deep into Pete's eyes to be sure he heard and understood every single word.

'We never lie to each other. We ask for what we want. We express what we need in ways that are clear and mature and work through our problems to make things work. Yes there's certain things we enjoy doing with and to each other that might seem weird to outsiders. Sick. Freakish. But we don't hurt each other.'

Slowly, Pete closed his hands over Dan's fingers. He unfurled them from his clothing one by one and Dan let him, stunned at the stiffness in his fists

'It's not like you to get physical, Dan.'

The observation collapsed the last of Dan's mood. 'I just want you to understand. I *need* you to understand. I would never, ever hurt her.'

The faintest trace of a smile tugged at the corner of Pete's lips. 'But you whip her, tie her up and keep her in a cage every now and then?'

A small smile, but it made all the difference. Dan backed away slightly. 'Sometimes.'

'You're bloody mad. And she likes it?'

'Loves it.'

'You know for sure?'

'Do you really think anybody could force Karen to do something she didn't want to do?'

Pete snickered. 'I'd love to see someone try.'

'Exactly. What we do is as normal as anything you get up to on a Saturday night.'

'My sex doesn't need props.' And just like that, the bubble of tension broke.

Dan picked up his beer and returned to the sofa. 'Maybe it should,' he smirked. 'When was the last time you had a shag anyway?'

'Fuck you.' Pete finally stopped frowning. 'So it's safe?'

'Always. SCS. *Safe. Consensual. Sane.* Nothing happens to anybody without us discussing it first and nothing is permanent. The marks were from a whip, but they'll be gone by tonight. I'd never hurt her, Pete. You must know that. Not just Karen, but anyone. I wouldn't hurt anybody for real.'

Pete had the good grace to look embarrassed. 'I know.'

The silence between them filled the room like smoke. Twenty seconds passed before Dan spoke again. 'Pete?'

'What?'

'I think I'm losing her.' The words left his mouth slowly and an ache filled his chest.

'I doubt it. A woman like Karen isn't going to let you strip her and stick her in a cage unless she's sticking around.'

'I'm serious. Mum really pissed her off. I need to show them both how serious I am. I can't take more days like this.'

Pete stared into the distance. 'How serious are you?'

With the question put plainly before him, Dan had to admit that he had no idea. Stalling, he rubbed his face with both hands, dragging the tips of his fingers across the stubble dotting his jaw. 'I don't want to lose her,' he said. 'I know that much.'

'You could marry her?'

He flinched, as though the very word was a slap across the face. 'And end up miserable like my parents? Fuck, no.'

A shadow of a smile crossed Pete's face. 'Your dad isn't miserable, is he?'

Sometimes Dan couldn't be sure. His father's weariness through the course of the afternoon matched other recent meetings, but he shied away from actually naming it miserable. Maybe just resigned and defeated?

'And your mum certainly isn't miserable. She loves having someone on hand to boss around all the time.'

'Exactly.'

'Not all married couples end up like that.'

'You're right. The ones that don't get divorced.' He shook his head. 'No. I won't do that to Karen or me.'

'But weddings are about commitment, right?'

'Weddings are about huge bills, stupid suits and tiny pieces of paper. They don't mean anything. Though it might be worth it just to see the look on Mum's face.' He enjoyed the mental image for a moment then shook his head.

'What then?'

'No idea. But if I don't do something it's all over. She's too smart to stick around if she's unhappy.'

'But *can* she dump you? Is that allowed?'

'Of course it is.'

'Sorry. I just don't get it. Karen could skin a grizzly just by looking at it, but you had her . . .'

'Caged?' Dan savoured the memory. Though he fought against it, his groin stirred at the thought of Karen kneeling and submissive behind those bars. Opening her mouth for him, sticking out her tongue so he could lay his cock against it.

A flush of red crept into Pete's neck and jaw. 'But you're in charge. How is she allowed to dump you?'

'We're just a normal couple.'

'No, you're not.'

'Okay, we're not. But that part is normal.'

'Then how does the dominant thing work?'

His mind drifted to her expectant expression as she waited for orders. The genuine passion in her face as he instructed her to suck him. 'I tell her to do something and she does. So long as I don't hit a hard limit it's free game.'

'And she's okay with that?'

'She has safe words if not. She says the words or makes the gesture and everything stops straight away.'

Pete snorted. 'Even in the middle?'

'Even in the middle. It's about respect. And trust.'

'I don't care what relationship I have, no woman should decide she doesn't like it right in the middle of shagging. What kind of tease is that?'

'Actually, it's quite exciting if done right.'

'You *are* crazy.' Though the words were hard, his smile returned and Pete took a swig from his neglected bottle. 'The pair of you. I mean that stick thing? It looks like it carries a charge.'

'The violet wand? It does.' Thinking back to the last time he used the wand brought a smile to Dan's lips. 'Big, purple sparks and crackling sounds like lightning. It's amazing.'

'Sparks? And it doesn't hurt?'

'More a tingle or a tickle. They have intensity settings. I can show you if you want?'

'You're not using that thing on me.'

'No, you silly bastard, on here.' He tugged his laptop from beneath the sofa.

Though he shook his head, Pete's gaze strayed to the laptop screen as Dan began to type. When the first video link opened, he leaned closer, eyes wide.

'Wow,' he murmured.

'I know.'

'And you can stick that bit inside her?' Pete pointed to a clear, curved attachment with a loose coil at one end.

'I could, but I don't have that one. We've got this though.' Dan clicked the next link.

Pete slapped his hand over his mouth. 'Fuck me!'

Dan grinned.

KAREN

Karen hid in the bedroom until she heard the front door close a second time. On venturing downstairs, she found Dan in the living room, his laptop open on the home page of a BDSM community forum. She watched him, following his search through various local girls and their pictures. Her stomach tightened and it took special effort to erase the mental image of hurling the laptop through the front room window. A quick cough brought his attention round to her.

'Hey.' He smiled.

She didn't return the affectionate gesture. 'Looking for more girls to fill your Library?'

'No.' He closed the laptop lid and pushed the machine to one side. 'I was showing Pete where we met.'

She glanced at the laptop, willing it to give up its secrets. 'Oh.'

'I had to. I know what I said about people finding out, but he was freaking out.' He didn't even look at her as he said it, his gaze focused near her shoulder. The rise and fall of his voice gave away his unease.

She stared, determined not to speak until he met her eyes. When he did, she held his stare and formed her words with deliberate slowness. 'Poor him.'

'Karen . . .'

'What about me? I was freaking out too.'

'I'm sorry.' He extended his hand, gesturing to the space beside him on the sofa. 'We need to talk.'

Instead of taking it, Karen sat on the single armchair on the other side of the room. 'Damn right we do. Your mum—'

'Don't. She's gone. Just drop it.'

'But she's awful Dan. She hates me and it sucks.'

'She doesn't hate *you*. She just wants what's best for me.'

Karen slapped her hand against her armrest. '*I'm* what's best for you. Just because she can't understand that doesn't mean she has the right to push me away.'

'You don't know the half of it.'

'What does that mean?'

'She tried to set me up with an old school friend.'

Karen gripped the arms of the chair. Her nails made dents in the worn faux leather. She enjoyed a few moments of fantasy, in which she pummelled Maxine's face with both fists before hearing Dan speak again.

'I told her no. I have you. I'm not interested in anyone else.'

Karen thought about Hannah, Rebecca, and other members of the Slave Library. She sighed. 'So you sent them away?'

'I sent *Mum* away. Dad followed. I don't know if they're still in Leicester, but I don't care. They're not staying here.'

And there it was. At last. A faint glimmer of "Dan The Dom" looking out for the interests of his sub. She smiled. 'Thanks.'

He nodded. 'Come here. Please?'

She slipped off the chair, on to the floor. A quick crawl took her across the carpet and up to Dan's legs where she rested her cheek on his knee. She shivered beneath his firm hand stroking down the nape of her neck. Tender fingers lifted the back of her vest. Traced a pattern over her shoulder blades.

'I'm sorry.'

'Why?'

'For Mum.'

Karen stiffened. 'Don't apologise for her. I don't need *your* apology for *her*.'

'Bloody hell, then what *do* you want?'

'I don't want to feel like I'm fighting her for you.'

'You're not.'

'She called and you ran off in the middle of a blowjob.' Saying it brought back the shock.

'She's my mum. I love her.'

'Fine, I get that, but what about me?'

Dan gazed at her helplessly. 'Don't ask me to choose.'

'I'm not. I just want you to respect the time we do have together. That's all.'

'But I love our time together.'

Karen flinched. She tasted blood on her tongue and realised she'd been gnawing her bottom lip. 'And me?'

'What about you?'

'How do you feel about me?' she prompted gently, forcing her voice into a vague approximation of nonchalance.

'You're my girlfriend. My slave. You mean so much to me. Sometimes I don't even believe you're real.'

She waited. After a few seconds, she sighed. 'Fine.'

'Why does that sound like "I give up"?'

Because it is, she thought. Aloud she said, 'No idea.'

Dan began to stroke her shoulders again. 'How's your back?'

'Pleasantly sore.'

'Good. You know, you never did finish that blowjob.'

'Whose fault is that?' she said, gnawing her bottom lip again.

Instead of answering Dan pulled his hand out of her vest and used it to unfasten his jeans. He touched the top of her head.

Karen considered jerking back. She imagined using one of her safe words and bringing Dan's hands to a fumbling halt. Then she saw the hungry look in his eyes and realised that she didn't want it to end. Ever. And that was the problem.

She licked her lips, followed his fingers as he reached into the gap of his boxers. Over the top of his waistband, Karen saw the head of his cock. Still soft, though showing signs of some hardness. She glanced over her shoulder. 'Pete's gone?'

'He saw the website, said something about a job in Beaumont Leys and ran off. Apparently all that porn is no preparation for the real thing.'

Giggling, Karen wrapped both hands around Dan's soft shaft and eased him free. She teased her fingers over the skin, watching the wrinkles smooth out as he hardened against her touch. 'I don't know why you showed him *Kink4Life*. That's not where we met. We met on *All SCS*.'

'No, we didn't.'

Karen ended the discussion by lowering her head to kiss Dan's swelling tip. He sucked in a sharp breath and tangled his fingers in her hair, drawing her closer. He didn't say anything. He didn't need to. His actions, his touch, all of it echoed with the return of "Dan The Dom;" from the easy confidence in his grip, to the low growl rumbling in the back of his throat. His true nature emerged as if from behind a curtain.

Pulling her knees more comfortably beneath her, Karen widened her mouth and put out her tongue. Dan eased himself in. A welcome tingle began between her legs and she dropped one hand past her jogging bottoms and into the front of her knickers. Slick moisture met her questing fingers.

Dan rolled his hips, initiating a gentle thrusting that Karen met with bobs of her head. A quick glance through her lashes showed her his closed eyes and sweaty forehead. She saw the pink tip of his tongue protrude from the side of his mouth and the quick rise and fall of his chest. The sight intensified the tingle across her pussy lips and brought more moisture. She swirled her fingers through it and listened to the hitches in his breathing. The low whimpers, trailing off into moans. His fingers tightened in her hair, just shy of painful. She flicked the tiny nub of sensitive flesh at the front of her opening and felt a thrill of pleasure shiver down her spine, through her legs and into her toes.

'You come first,' Dan whispered.

Karen lifted her head. 'What?'

'Don't stop.' He used her hair to yank her back into place. He pushed deep into her throat and held her steady. 'Just listen. You come first. It's a present. Thank me later.'

As her pleasure-addled mind tried to take it in, Karen relaxed her throat. His firm cock slid farther back and she concentrated on suppressing her gag reflex. When comfortable, she put out her tongue and let him slide back and forth across it. The penetration made her struggle for breath, bringing in a rush of light-headedness that sparked stars before her eyes. She put her hand on Dan's knee, with her middle fingers pressed down against her palm. He pulled back slightly, but didn't release her hair. In fact, his grip tightened, twisting the curly strands at their roots. The sharp pain mingled with pleasure until Karen lost all sense of which was which.

'Are you okay?' His voice was gruff. Unsteady. 'Do you need a break?'

Just hearing him speak in such a way soothed her jangled nerves. It brought a feeling of safety and security to her mind that simultaneously confused and excited her. How could he be so perfect in one moment and so utterly infuriating in the next? Stinging pain lanced through her scalp.

'Well?' Dan insisted.

Karen extended her index finger, the silent signal for "no."

'You sure?'

In answer, she lunged forward, impaling herself on his cock again. She tasted a tiny drop of precum and swallowed, working her throat muscles until Dan began to tremble beneath her.

'Okay, Kaz.' He twisted his hips slightly. 'You first, remember. Hurry up.'

But Karen didn't hurry up. She took her hand from her knickers and used the dampness on her fingers to massage the skin beneath Dan's cock. The slippery skin drew taut and pulled upward, bringing his testicles with them. Loud groans slid from his mouth, chased by a rough, animal panting.

'Kaz, please.' The mask of "Dan The Dom" slipped to reveal the man beneath. The one who, despite all her assurances, still expressed guilt over his need to control.

Karen worked hard to send that man away, humming around her mouthful of cock. A surge of delight fizzed through her limbs from neck to toes as Dan moaned and tilted his head back once more. His eyes rolled back in his head. A pitch change; high to low and he cried out, pulling on her hair again. *Not enough*, she thought. *More. He needs more.*

Ignoring her own discomfort, Karen sank down until dark curls of pubic hair tickled the space beneath her eyelids. The hot, thick length of him stretched her wide, but she swallowed anyway, massaging him with her throat muscles. She tucked her hands beneath her chin to grip his balls and squeeze.

'Fuck . . .' he whimpered.

The frantic jerking of Dan's hips told Karen to hold back. She slowed the motions of her mouth and released his cock from the depths of her throat to lick and kiss the hot, stiff length. The free hand went back to her knickers. Two fingers slid into her slippery folds while her thumb lingered on the sensitive skin of her clit. She became aware of her own breathing, quick, irregular and shallow. Sweat pasted the vest to her back and stung the sensitive skin where flog marks remained. *Still not enough.* A third finger slipped past her pussy lips to join the first two. Her thumb maintained constant pressure where she needed it most.

'Damn it, Karen,' Dan choked. 'Hurry up.'

The wet squelch of her thrusting fingers drowned out his voice. Eyes closed, lips once more forming a tight seal around Dan's rod, she concentrated on the feeling of tight, tingling warmth oozing out from her belly. It flushed every inch of skin. Made her limbs tremble like a guttering candle flame. Numb warmth started at the tips of her toes and crawled forward through her feet and up her legs.

'Damn you, Kaz, what did I say?'

Karen had just time to recognize the command in his voice before Dan grabbed her by the chin and heaved her mouth away from his cock. Dizzy, breathless, Karen went limp as he pulled her across his lap with her face turned to the ceiling, legs dangling. She felt the rigid length of his cock press into her ribs and moaned through clenched teeth. That's what she wanted. Craved. Needed as surely as air.

Her body arched when Dan grabbed her breasts. He squeezed them through the vest then pinched each nipple until her moans turned into yelps of pain.

Karen kept thrusting with her fingers. She closed her eyes, though not before she saw him lean forward. Then his teeth fastened on the exposed line of flesh between her neck and shoulder. He bit down and Karen screamed a low, quivering note. Pain met pleasure and the pair crashed together with an impact that left spots of white dancing behind her closed eyelids. Her fingers spasmed inside her body and wave after wave of delicious release rolled through her body and flattened her sense of reason.

'That's better,' Dan spoke through teeth still clenched on a mouthful of flesh. 'When I say you first, I mean it. Understand?' The word ended on a growl.

Karen jerked her hand from her underwear and stuffed the sticky fingers into her mouth one by one. Ecstasy flowed through her body from her pussy outward across every inch of skin. Tremors shot through her limbs and made her pull against Dan's teeth. Still unsteady, she offered no complaint as he released his grip. The room spun as he turned her over. His cock pressed into her stomach, but before that fresh pleasure had time to register, Dan pulled her jogging bottoms down. Then her underwear. He spanked her bare cheek. She winced. Cool air caressed her arse.

'Do. You. Un. Der. Stand?' He marked each syllable with a firm slap to her arse.

'Yes, Sir,' she moaned, grinding her clit against his jeans.

'Good. Now finish me off.' He kissed the sore patches on each cheek and let her roll off his lap.

As her mind and body wandered back toward each other over the abyss of pleasure, Karen sank to her knees. She smiled, conscious of the damp dribbles running down her thigh. Still fuzzy and jelly-legged, she dragged her sluggish body into position between Dan's legs.

The head of his cock pointed at her face, wet and quivering. She slurped it back into her mouth and immediately felt Dan respond by twitching against her tongue. Again he tangled his fingers in her hair and this time he kept control, using his grip to jerk her face up and down while thrusting with his hips.

'Yes,' he hissed. 'God yes. Fucking suck me. Finish it.'

The filthy expression on Dan's face, coupled with his guttural breathing dragged Karen back to the brink. She put a hand back between her legs and caressed the hypersensitive skin. The other massaged Dan's tightening balls.

He tensed and bit his lip. 'Yes, don't move. I'm nearly there . . .'

A phone rang. The clanging bells and grating voice of the Crazy Frog filled the room and Karen bolted upright, leaving several hairs wrapped around Dan's clutching fingers.

'No!' he shouted.

Dan's hips rocked forward, his backside rearing off the sofa as he finally gave in. His own orgasm clawed keening groans from the depths of his throat and long strings of sticky, white semen arced through the air. Some struck his stomach and slid down his shirt like sexually charged snail trails. The rest splattered the lid of his laptop.

'Damn it, Kaz!' He growled through a series of laboured pants. 'It's not funny.'

She stared at his laptop and the creamy trails oozing into the housing. 'I'm so sorry.'

'Then stop laughing.'

'I can't!' Snickering, Karen crawled across the room and snatched her phone from the coffee table. She held it to her ear. 'Hi, Cindy.'

'Everything is shit and everyone sucks!' said the hysterical voice at the other end.

'What happened?'

'Sam dumped me.'

The laughter died as though it had never been. Still tingling and breathless from the powerful orgasm, Karen took a second to steady herself. She wiped the sticky hand on her vest and pushed her hair off her forehead. She pulled her underwear and jogging bottoms up to rest on her hips.

'When?' She waved aside Dan's questioning look and perched on the single armchair.

'Just now. An hour ago. I don't know. I started the rum when I got off the phone. It's gone now.'

'I'm sorry, honey.'

'Come home, Kaz. I need you.'

Karen looked at Dan. Smirked at the sight of him gingerly scoping spunk off his laptop. 'I can't.'

'Don't leave me here alone.'

'I'm supposed to spend tonight with Dan.'

'He's more important than me?'

Karen rolled her eyes and walked open-eyed into the guilt-trap. 'You know he's not.'

'Then come home. Help me finish the other bottle.'

'Give me half an hour.' Sighing, she hung up.

Dan glared at her. 'We need to talk about your blowjob technique. And your bloody ringtone.'

'I only use it for Cindy; it guarantees I'll answer.'

'It's annoying as hell. What did she want?'

'It's Sam.'

'Again?' Dan stopped wiping. 'What set them off this time?'

'Don't know, but I need to help her.'

'Right. You can run off to help your friend, but I can't pick up my parents?'

Karen pressed her fingers against her eyelids. Red spots danced across her vision when she let go. 'Don't be a dick. You know this is different.'

'How?'

'You're not in a cage. You got to come. Cindy isn't a complete bitch who hates your guts.' She counted each point on her fingers. 'We've finished playing as far as I can tell. I could keep going.'

Dan opened his mouth again. When she pinned him with a firm look, he pressed his lips together and returned to wiping the laptop.

Karen raised her key to the door but it opened before she could insert it. Instead of the hallway, she saw a tumbler of pale amber liquid, held at eye height. Several ice cubes clinked against the bottom.

'Here.' Cindy stood on the other side of the glass, tall, skinny and bald but for a crest of ice-white hair flowing down the centre of her head to the small of her back. She wore nothing but tattoos, a cropped vest over tiny white panties, and an expression like that of a kicked puppy. 'Take it then.'

Karen blinked at the glass before plucking it from Cindy's shaking hand. When her friend fixed her with an expectant stare, she tilted her head and downed the liquid in one gulp. The sting of alcohol and a tiny chip of ice made her cough. 'Can I come in now?'

'I guess.' Cindy spun on her heel and marched into the flat.

Karen followed her over the threshold and shut the door. In the living room, Cindy flopped cross-legged on to the floor beside a small tin of weed. She formed a fat, lumpy roll from a wide piece of sticky paper and a pinch from the tin. Sucking hard, she held a flickering match to one end. 'Want some?'

Karen wrinkled her nose. 'No and neither should you. It stinks in here.'

'Don't care. Makes me feel better.'

A flick of her wrist tossed her bag beneath the coffee table. Next, Karen sank into the rustling embrace of a tatty purple beanbag. She placed the empty tumbler on the floor. 'Well?'

'If I can't be honest with my family then this relationship has nowhere to go.' Cindy made air quotes with her fingers.

'Sam said that? Really?' When Cindy nodded a second time, Karen reached out to hold her.

She swayed out of reach and sucked harder on the joint. 'It's not fair. I've tried, but it's not easy.'

'What happened?'

'We had dinner at Mum's house. She asked about Sam and I just froze. My brain jammed. In the end I said we were work colleagues.'

Karen winced. 'Bet that went well.'

'You think?'

Karen slid off the beanbag and put her arm around Cindy's shoulders in what she hoped was a comforting way. 'This is your first serious relationship in forever. It's a big deal. And I know it's hard, but you have to tell them eventually. You can't hide it forever.'

'Oh, yeah?'

'It's not fair to Sam.'

Cindy's expression crumpled. 'You think I don't know that? Every time we meet it's the same. "When are you going to tell them?" "Have you told them yet?" "What are you waiting for?"'

'Sounds like a lot of pressure.'

'It is! You know I don't deal well with pressure.' Cindy sucked her blunt and spat a cloud of smoke into the air. Her shoulders slumped. 'I end up smoking these.'

'Does Sam know?'

'Probably. You're right, it stinks. Can't really hide it.' After flapping her hand at the smoke a few times, she crossed to the window and yanked it open. A breath of air billowed through, laced with the scent of car exhaust and grease from the fast food chicken place three doors down.

Sensing refuge, Karen scrambled up and crossed to the window. A few coughs later she spoke again. 'What now?'

'No idea. Get drunk or get laid, I guess.'

'You don't mean that.'

'Oh yeah?' Cindy paced around the room until she reached the bottle of rum. She refilled her glass, gulped it down, and then repeated the motion before topping up Karen's. 'If she can't understand what a big deal this is, then why should I keep chasing her?'

'She does understand, but *you* need to understand what *she's* going through. It can't be easy dating a pothead when you're a copper— talk about conflict of interests. Add that to the fact that she's a girl *and* gay in a man's profession . . . she just needs the same commitment from you.'

'Whose side are you on?'

'I just want to give you the other side of the argument. Think about how she feels.'

'What about me? I hate lying, but imagine the conversation with my wannabe Nazi parents. They have a hard enough time with you.'

Though she chuckled, Karen understood. She felt a prickle of unease tease down her spine at the memory of her last visit to the Smith household.

'How's your mum?'

Cindy scratched the flaming heart tattooed across her right shoulder. 'She stopped scrubbing the sofa cushions, if that's what you mean.'

Karen cocked an eyebrow.

'I'm exaggerating, but I don't think she's ever had a black woman in her house before. I won't take you there again. Sam neither. Mum would disown me for sure.'

'But you're so happy.'

'As if that means anything!' Cindy's fingers tightened on the shortening stub of her blunt. 'Sam and I don't fit into Mum's perfect little world of boy-girl couples who marry, *then* have sex. And have six brat kids. I've told Sam this, but she still wants me to come out.'

At a loss for what else to do, Karen returned to her tumbler and held it aloft. 'To crazy-arse mother figures.'

'Here, here.' Cindy drained her glass. Refilled it. 'What's up with your mum?'

'Nothing. Dan's mum is a nightmare.'

'She can't be worse than mine.'

Karen snorted. 'Today, she tried to set Dan up with another woman.'

'Bitch.'

Having her own words repeated back at her eased some of the ache in Karen's mind. 'She thinks I'm after his money.'

'Dan's a social worker. He doesn't have any money.'

'No, but Maxine does.'

Cindy looked vague.

'She's a bit famous. She starred in some stupid sitcom in the seventies, *Home with Mr. Barclay*? She's got loads stashed away and no other kids. What else will she do with it when she pops it?'

'You've thought this through. She should be worried.'

'Shut up, ho-bag!' She aimed a playful punch at Cindy's arm.

In the pause that followed, Cindy finished her smoke. She pulled the last few dregs out of the stub, and then flicked it in the direction of a plant pot on the other side of the room. Waving at the lingering clouds of smoke, she retrieved the rum bottle and drank directly from the neck.

'Fuck this.' Cindy burped and gestured with the bottle. 'Let's go out.'

'Seriously? It's a Thursday.'

'Can't you go out on a school night?'

'Screw you.' Karen displayed the back of her middle finger.

'You wish. Come out with me. You don't have to be at the university until next Friday. Come have some fun.'

'I'm not sure.'

'You scared of fun now?'

'No.'

Cindy swigged from the bottle again. 'Then come out with me.'

Karen took in her friend's unfocused gaze and swaying stance. 'No, and you shouldn't either. Call Sam. Talk to her.'

'No.'

'You guys just need to talk it through.'

'Like you and Dan?' Cindy snorted. 'Because you've been so good about telling him to stick his stupid Slave Library.'

Smart-arse retorts froze on Karen's tongue. She turned away from the window and back towards the room. She looked not at her friend, but at the floor, nibbling her bottom lip. 'I like the Slave Library.'

'And I secretly love cock.' Cindy snapped. 'Are you still kidding yourself? I know he's blind, so he won't see it, but you should know yourself better than that.'

'I don't know what you mean.'

Cindy sighed and shook her head. 'I'm going out. If you feel like joining me, I'll be at Helsinki.'

The thought of Cindy loose in one of the biggest, noisiest gay clubs around almost made Karen change her mind. 'Please stay in,' she whispered. 'We'll watch Resident Evil. You can perv on Mila Jovovitch.'

'Nice try. I'm getting changed.'

Fifteen minutes later, Cindy emerged from her room wearing scruffy dungarees over a fishnet bodysuit and Doc Marten boots. She lingered near the door. 'Last chance.'

It was tempting— so tempting. Perhaps it would be nice to blow off some steam. To dance. To drink. Fondle a stranger beneath some garish blue and green strobe lighting.

She shook her head. 'No thanks.'

'Whatever. Don't wait up.' Cindy slammed the door behind her.

Karen sat in the silence and tried to pull her thoughts under control. In the end, she dropped to her knees and pummelled the beanbag until her hair stuck to her face and her breath rasped through her lungs.

Leaving the rum and the other debris of Cindy's distress, she rushed into her room, flung open the doors of her wardrobe and reached for the back. Her fingers touched the smooth surface of her vibrator and dragged it into the open. Karen peeled off her clothes. Dived beneath the duvet. Switched on massager at its lowest setting and shoved it between her legs.

The dull hum soon eclipsed all other sounds in the flat but for the low whistle of her own breathing. Soon, the hum took on a fresh pitch as Karen's body reacted to the stimuli. She pressed the round, vibrating head harder against her clit and closed her eyes. Her free hand roamed, stroking, poking, pinching, twisting. Erect nipples stood out beneath her fingers, teased to stiff points by the soft brush of the cotton duvet. A damp patch formed on the sheets beneath her.

Next setting. The buzz grew higher. Her free hand played over her stomach and breasts before shifting up to her throat. Then her questing fingers found the patch of flesh still aching from Dan's incredible bite a short while before. Her clit swelled with a fresh rush of sensitising blood and she moaned into the pillows.

Dan . . . Master . . .

She imagined him beside her, replacing her hands with his. She remembered the stab of pain from his teeth and tried to recreate it by pinching the same area. Just as the familiar pressure began to build the vibrator gave a grumbling whine and switched itself off. Her pleasure guttered on its upward incline and slid back down into nothing.

Karen's eyes popped open. 'Fuck.'

A quick jerk removed the back panel and she tipped the four dead batteries into her palm.

Not for the first time, she vowed to buy a new vibrator with a plug attachment.

She wrapped the duvet around her body, left the spent toy on the mattress, and wandered back into the living room. Her body tingled with left over pleasure and the scratch of cotton against her bare skin made her shiver.

A burst of icy cold swirled against her legs and thighs as she opened the freezer in search of ice cream.

Mint chocolate chip. Rum and raisin.

Karen took both and a spoon off the draining board before heading back to her room. Half way there, she heard a dull buzz and the muted tones of "Slave 4U" from the depths of her handbag.

The phone, when she eventually unearthed it, displayed "Master Calling" to match the ring tone she used for Dan's calls. Her thumb hovered over the connect button. The phone stopped ringing. She considered calling back but the memory of Cindy's voice filled her head again. Accusing. Damning. Irritatingly correct.

'I hate the Library,' she told the silent phone. 'I hate that I have to share you all the time. With other girls, your mum— why can't you just be mine?'

It rang again.

Karen hugged the ice cream tubs tighter to her body and dropped the little machine on the sofa.

Not now.

Backing away from the sofa and the phone, she returned to her bedroom and shut the door.

DAN

Dan raised the volume on the TV and spread his legs. His flaccid cock flopped against his thigh and on grasping it he felt no stirrings there. He grunted and began to rub it, gaze pinned to the naked, skinny, blonde woman on screen, kneeling before a man dressed head to toe in customary black.

She licked her lips and thumbed her breasts in a provocative display of submission then opened her mouth. As soon as the Dom's cock touched her tongue, she began an excessive sequence of grinding, writhing, and moaning, all while fingering herself with long, French manicured nails.

He turned off the TV. Never before had he realised how ridiculous most porn was. His mind strayed to Karen and the soft smoothness of her skin beneath his fingers as they watched such movies together. He remembered her hands mimicking the actions on screen and the heat of her breath against his ear.

In the space on the sofa usually reserved for her, lay a box of tissues, four empty lager bottles, a bag of crisps, and a tube of KY. Yet again he picked up his mobile and picked "Kaz Kitten" from the top of the recently called list.

The line rang and rang and rang. When her chirpy voice pitched in with its pre-recorded message, Dan wiped his eyes with the tips of his fingers. 'Kaz,' he said after the beep, 'it's me. Dan. Daniel. Again. Please call me. I'm sorry. I'm watching the DVDs you got me for Christmas, but they're really shit. Like really, really, really shit. Why did you buy me shit DVDs?' He burped. 'I can't even get it up without you here. You always make it fun when we watch these movies. Why won't you answer your phone?'

Eventually, even through the mind-fuzz of too much alcohol, he realised there was nothing more to say. He hung up and placed the phone on the floor near his foot beside several wads of damp tissue. Snagging a fresh lager from the pack on the coffee table, he popped the lid and drank.

When the landline rang he had to try twice to leave the sofa.

The room lurched and the carpet wobbled beneath his feet, but he made it to the wall without falling and plucked the handset off the hook. 'Karen, is that you?'

'We made it home safely, darling. Just thought you'd like to know.'

He frowned. 'What?'

'It's me. Mummy, darling.'

He burped and tasted old lager. 'Oh, you . . .'

'Yes, we're back in Ely. We got a train straight back. It's a good thing we had open tickets.'

'Good. Okay.' He clutched the wall, the receiver rammed against his ear while his mind raced, searching for excuses to hang up.

After long seconds of silence, Maxine spoke again. 'You really surprised me today, Daniel. I taught you better than that.'

'Better than what?' he slurred, thinking back over his behaviour that evening. Nothing in his memories deserved this scolding.

'Better than to treat your father and I in such a way.'

'I treat Dad just fine. You're the one I booted from the house.'

'Daniel!'

'What?' Leaning against the wall, he hissed down the phone. 'You did it to yourself. You come unannounced. You insult my girlfriend and my friend. And me. You insin—insinu—'

'Insinuate?'

'Insinuate that Karen and Pete are fucking about behind my back and try to shove a some ancient nursery bimbo into my life.' He heard her gasp and rode right over it. 'You're ruining my relationship. And that's not fair.'

'Darling, are you drunk?'

'Yes,' he said with self-righteous enthusiasm. 'I reckon so. And that's your fault too.' That felt even better.

'That's not fair, darling.'

'Life isn't fair. You taught me that when you bought my cousin an electronic bike for Christmas and all I got was a jumper with cows on.'

'You liked cows.'

'Whatever.'

'I want to talk about Karen.'

He gripped the phone until the plastic creaked. 'Oh, well done, Mum. Now you know her name? After you've messed everything up.'

'Daniel, stop being so flighty.'

'No, *you* stop interfering. I don't want to talk about Karen. Not with you. I want you to be happy for us. If you can't do that, leave us alone.'

'Darling—'

'No. That's it. I said it.' Acknowledging the words brought a sense of calm to his mind. It steadied the writhing of his stomach and warmed his chest. He actually smiled. 'It's done. I mean it. Be happy or leave us alone.'

A faint sniff issued from the handset. 'Is that really what you want?'

'Yes, damn it.'

'I thought my only son would have more love for his mother, but—'

He sighed. 'Don't do that. I'm too drunk to handle your games tonight.'

'What games?'

'Your "Poor me, the whole world is out to get me" game. Your "If I keep picking at his girlfriend maybe he'll dump her" game.'

'Darling, you're tired. You should go to bed—'

'Stop it! Don't mother-smother me now. I don't need it, I have Karen.' Even through the booze-fog Dan realised he'd caught onto something. If his mother's sharp intake of breath wasn't clue enough, her next words cinched it.

'That girl? She rents a flat but stays in your house whenever she feels like it, eating your food without paying any bills. She's no good for you. She can't take care of you. You'll always need your mother for that.'

He laughed. 'Jesus, I get it now. You can't stand that I might need her more than you.'

'You're drunk.' Maxine's voice no longer simpered. It snapped and cracked like ice cubes breaking. 'I won't talk to you when you're drunk.'

'*You* phoned *me*.'

'For a sensible conversation—'

'To squish me back under your thumb.' More laughter, and a small hiccup that turned into another burp part way through. 'I should talk to you while drunk more often. You actually make more sense that way.'

'Daniel, please—'

'I'm hanging up now.'

'Wait a moment, darling, I don't think—'

Dan pressed his forehead against phone, depressing the button at the top.

In the silence that followed Dan waited for the sense of liberation and pleasure to take over. It didn't. Instead he felt a rush of nausea that sent him racing for the stairs. Half way there he realised, with his last shred of sense, that he would never make it to the bathroom.

Heaving, he dashed for the kitchen, hung his head over the sink, and let his stomach go, eyes closed to avoid splatter. Four bottles of lager and most of the crisps hit the bottom of the sink. He waited until the last tremors past then turned on the tap, swirling the chunks down the plug hole. Stubborn lumps clung to the sides. Rather than fighting with it, Dan trudged back to the living room and to his phone. He pressed redial. 'Karen?' he whispered. 'Please call me. Please.'

That done, he called Pete.

His friend answered on the third ring. 'I'm not coming back over there.'

'You don't need to.'

'You sure? You've not handcuffed her to the radiator or swung her from the light fixture?'

Despite himself, Dan laughed. 'I use rope for that. No need for keys.'

Pete grunted. 'You're not kidding are you?'

'Nope.'

'What do you want, mate?'

'I need help—'

'Yeah?'

'With Karen. I'm sitting here watching *Paid in Manhattan* and I can't even—'

'Wait, just stop. Please tell me you haven't called me in the middle of a wank. I'm not part of your weird, kinky shit.'

Dan looked away from the pile of dirty tissues. 'No. I mean I was, but I'm finished now.'

'Jesus . . .'

'Will you listen to me, for a second, please? I need your help.'

'Wanking?'

'No. Drag your head out of the gutter. It's not all about sex.'

'Could have fooled me.'

'This was stupid. I shouldn't have called you.' He took the phone away from his ear.

'No, wait, wait. I'm sorry. You surprised me, that's all. Hello? Dan?'

'What?'

'I'm here. Tell me what's wrong.'

Dan sighed. 'My girlfriend hates me. My mum hates my girlfriend.'

'I'm up to speed on all that.'

'I can't get through to Karen.'

'She's not with you?'

He glanced again at the empty space on the sofa. 'She went home.'

'That's rough. Sorry.'

'No, hang on, we've not split up.' Even as he spoke the words, a knot formed in his stomach. His knees quivered.

Had they? Until that moment he hadn't considered the possibility.

'Why would you assume that?' he whispered.

'You said she went home.'

'She doesn't live here.'

Pete gave a non-committal grunt. 'She may as well. She's always there from what I can tell.'

'We haven't split up.'

'You sure about that?'

Dan bit his lip. 'I've left her about six messages. And texts. She won't answer the phone. What does that mean?'

'Hell if I know.'

'Help me out here.' Desperation gave his voice a trembling quality. 'I have to do something.'

'Like what? As you kindly reminded me earlier, I've not got my rocks off for months. I'm the wrong person to hit for advice.'

'You must have some ideas.'

'Take her somewhere nice and show her you care.' He put sarcastic emphasis on the words. 'All that romantic crap.'

'Like flowers? Chocolates?'

Pete snickered. 'Buy her chocolate and she'll eat you alive. Come on, think about it. You and Karen have something. Make it personal.'

'Personal?' He frowned at the empty room.

'Something important to the two of you, not some generic store-bought shit.'

Dan slumped onto the sofa and stared at the ceiling. He saw the small holes in the plaster from failed attempts to install suspension hooks. 'Well . . .'

'What does she like?'

'I don't know. Test tubes?'

'What the hell?'

'She did a chemistry degree.'

'Fuck me, you suck. Okay, what about those books she was reading last year? The fantasy ones on TV now? Or that comedian she likes? Try something to do with them.'

'Comedian?'

'The tall one with the long hair.'

He shrugged. Seconds later, when he realised the gesture was pointless, Dan spoke aloud. 'No idea.' He sat up. Though the strain of recently vomiting left an ache in his throat, his thoughts were the clearest they'd been in hours. 'But how do you know all this stuff about Karen?'

'Dunno,' Pete cleared his throat.

'Even her folks don't know her that well. She told me her dad bought her a gold watch for Christmas last year.'

'She hasn't worn gold since she was a teenager.'

'Exactly.' Dan sat very still. He listened to the low breathing on the other end of the phone and the low murmurs from *Paid in Manhattan* still playing in the background. He turned it off. 'So, what else you got?'

'She's *your* girlfriend, mate.' Pete's tone flattened. 'Your *slave* or whatever it is.'

'Yes, but—'

'Then *you* do the fucking legwork.'

'Wow, Pete.' Stunned, he raised his hand as if to ward off the fire he heard raging in his friend's voice. 'Okay. Fine. I'll sort it. Thanks, I guess.'

'Whatever.' He hung up.

Dan stared at the phone. *What the fuck was that about?*

Undeniably sober now, he set the phone on the coffee table well out of reach. Though part of him longed to analyse Pete's peculiar mood swing, the rest of him yearned to deal with the more pressing problem of his love life. His grumpy, sex-starved friend would have to wait.

He retrieved his laptop from beneath the sofa. Just touching it reminded him of the last time he used it, and the creamy trails of Karen's hard work sinking into the gaps beneath the casing. Several of the keys stuck as he logged on.

Personal, he thought, signing into his usual forum, *I can do personal.*

KAREN

Karen lifted her head. Her pillow peeled away from her cheek with a dull, tearing sound and stood up in a stiff peak. Drool and sticky patches of another bodily fluid matted the white cotton. She groaned and clamped her hands over her ears to cut out the dawn chorus.

Two ice cream tubs lay beside the empty bottle of rum. A small pool of melted mint-chocolate chip and an open pack of AA batteries reminded Karen of the previous night.

Rolling out of bed, she pushed the door open and peered into the dark hallway. If Cindy's closed door told an obvious story, then the two sets of snores pouring through it gave the epilogue.

She shook her head. The hallway faded in and out of focus, and her stomach gave a lurch strong enough to assure her that sudden movements were a bad idea. In the kitchen she slammed bread into the toaster and filled the kettle while trying not to think. Her pounding head made that easier than she might have liked. Coffee didn't help. Toast did, thickly smeared with honey to hide the smell and taste of carbon. Chewing slowly, Karen retrieved her phone from the sofa where she'd thrown it hours earlier.

Twenty-six missed calls. Twelve voice mails. Six text messages. Karen read them one by one and, with each message, felt her stomach clench. 'Oh, Dan.' Her lower lip wobbled. She listened to the voice mail messages and laughed while tears streamed down her cheeks.

'You're such a stupid drunk,' she whispered. Her thumb hovered over "Compose Message," but before she could begin, she heard footsteps approach from the hallway. She spun around, prepared to give Cindy a piece of her mind. She stopped dead. 'Sam?'

'Yeah.' Short, with miraculously neat hair, Sam sidled into the kitchen. She wore a pair of Cindy's pyjamas, stretched taut over her curvy hips and chest. She kicked a chubby leg over one of the stools at the breakfast bar and sat down. 'What?'

'You spent the night here?'

'Yep.'

'With Cindy?'

'I hope so.'

Karen widened her eyes. 'I thought you dumped her?'

Sam shrugged and pointed to the toast. Karen pushed the plate over and watched the other woman crunch through several mouthfuls.

'Ugh, what's wrong with you two? Cindy has her toast burnt to all hell too.'

'It's a shitty toaster. Talk to me, Sam. I thought you two were done.'

'We were. Then I realised I really do love her.'

She nodded. 'But when did you get here?'

'I brought her home at about 4 a.m.'

'Don't you work Thursdays?'

'Yep.'

When the implications of that monosyllabic answer sank in, Karen swore and put her head in her hands.

'Good. I'm glad you get it.' Sam stopped munching the toast long enough to glare. 'Why the hell didn't you go with her? She was higher than a kite.'

'What did she do?'

'Kicked some guy in the nads for hitting on her. Then robbed another guy when he tried to buy her a drink.'

She winced. 'Is she in trouble?'

'No, but only because I stepped in. Then again, that first guy was a prick. Not that I condone assault – of course – but good for her.'

They shared a smile.

'Anyway, some woman found her trying to flag down a cab by waving her bra at passing cars. I took over and brought her back here. It was the end of my shift anyway. Thankfully.'

'I'm so sorry. I should have gone with her. I know that. I just couldn't face it.'

'It's that bad with Dan?'

Karen looked up from her toast. Heat flooded her cheeks. 'I—'

'She told me.' Sam's expression softened. She gave a tiny smile full of pity.

'Right.' Karen cleared her throat. 'Dan and I need to talk, yes, but it's no excuse. I should have been there for Cindy.'

'Don't worry about it. She's fine. Woke right up when I tried to strip her down for bed. She's a biter now. Apparently.' Sam lifted her pyjama top, showing off a large bruise forming on the side of her left breast.

Thinking of her own bruised neck, Karen hid a smile behind her hand. 'So you're okay now? You and Cindy?'

Sam nodded.

'What about her parents?'

'Fuck them.' The answer came not from Sam, but Cindy herself who appeared in the doorway wearing nothing but faint smears of body glitter and a wide smile. 'I'm happy. So is Sam. Everyone else can fuck right off.'

Karen beamed.

'You coming back to bed, or what?'

For several confusing seconds, Karen thought the question was directed at her. Then she saw Sam stand, stretch and amble back toward the bedroom, dodging a poorly aimed slap at her backside as she went. 'Don't keep me waiting,' she said.

Alone with her friend, Karen chuckled. 'You're something else.'

Cindy gave an exaggerated flick of her ice-white hair. 'I do my best.'

'I'm so sorry, Cindy.'

'What for?'

'For leaving you alone. I should have gone with you. That was shitty of me.'

'Yep. Bitch.'

She looked up, ready to snap back with a matching insult. The words died on her tongue. 'I deserved that.'

'Yes, but I get it. Your relationship is hard, too.'

'You sure you're okay?'

Cindy spread her hands. 'No assault charges. Minimal hangover. Fucking sexy copper waiting in my bedroom. Yeah, I'm fine.'

'Good.'

'You will be too, Kaz.'

'I'm not so sure.'

'Then take your own advice. Call Dan. Talk to him.'

Karen thought back to all those missed calls and voice mails. 'I don't know if I can.'

'You have to. Suck it up. Be honest and tell him how you feel.'

'I have.'

'Not about his mum, about how *you feel*. It's not the same. He already knows you don't like her. But have you told him that what she says makes you feel insecure?'

'I'm not insecure.'

'Bullshit. We've been friends too long; don't lie to me as well as yourself. You feel insecure. You may like playing with other girls occasionally but you hate this Slave Library. You're worried he's doing it because he also thinks you're not good enough. Worse still, you don't know where the relationship is going. Is it just D/s fun to him or is there more? *You* want more.'

No matter how hard she tried, Karen couldn't think of a decent response. She pressed her lips together. 'I love him so much.' She lost the battle to keep her lower lip from wobbling. 'I know it's not been that long, not like you and Sam, but I do. I can see us together years from now. He's perfect.'

Tears gathered in her eyes. She blinked them away with the palms of her hands. Despite the implications of the word "perfect" Karen couldn't think of a better one. Of all her past relationships, Dan was the only one who managed to blend kink with vanilla in a way that worked. He understood her need to submit came not from a troubled or abused past, but from a need to relax. To trade off the control she demanded in every other aspect of her life in exchange for pleasure shared.

Love. Such a loaded word, but it made sense here. Nothing else fit the pounding of her heart each time he touched her or the gentle warmth in her belly when he smiled. Or even the giddy flush of pride that suffused her heart every time he introduced her as "my girlfriend."

Sam stepped deeper into the room and placed a hand on her shoulder. 'I know, honey.'

'He can't even say it. He's never told me he loves me. I'm "important" to him. He "loves our time together".' The words tasted as bitter as they sounded, heavy with disappointment and frustration.

'He's a man. They suck at the best of times, but he seems worse.'

'He's just cautious.'

'No, he's hurting you. And if he keeps it up, I'll break his legs. But talk to him first, okay? Sam can't keep blagging me out of trouble.'

Karen laughed through her tears. Throughout all the drama in her life Karen knew she could depend on Cindy to be vulgar, coarse, and most of all, honest.

'Sure,' she whispered. 'Thanks.'

'No problem.' Cindy turned toward her room. 'Now get out of my house.'

'It's my house too.'

'I'm using it with my dirty playmate. So get out, unless you're joining us.'

Karen laughed. 'Put some clothes on, you slut.'

'Why? She'll just tear them off me again.' Cindy walked away, putting a little sway into her hips as she went.

At Dan's front door, Karen took a deep breath, squared her shoulders, and knocked. A few seconds later, the door opened.

'Kaz. Thank God. Why didn't you use your key?'

'I need to talk to you.'

'Me too.'

Heart thudding a little harder at those two simple words, she allowed Dan to guide her over the threshold.

Sweaty palms. She wiped them on her jeans and declined the offer of tea. Instead she sat on the edge of the sofa and put her hands in her lap.

Dan sat opposite her on the single seat. 'I called you.'

'I know.

'I left messages.'

'I know.' Guilt dropped her voice to a low whisper.

'You could have— why didn't you—' He rubbed his face. Something about his voice sounded rough and grainy, like sandpaper. His stained dressing gown hung loose off one shoulder and a tuft of dark hair stuck up from the side of his head.

'You look like shit,' she murmured.

'I *feel* like shit. You scared me. I thought that was it.'

'I'm sorry.'

'All those calls. Why didn't you answer?'

'I don't know. I was angry. I didn't know what to say.' She stared at her shoes.

'Karen, you can't do that to me. You can't just— damn it.'

'You were drunk. There's no way we could have had a sensible conversation.'

'I was fine after I threw up in the sink.'

'The sink?' She wrinkled her nose. 'Gross, Dan.'

He shrugged. 'I cleaned it.'

'Still gross.'

'I know. And I know what a pain my mum is. I shouldn't have brought her here. And I shouldn't have left you in that cage. I fucked up a lot yesterday.'

'Damn right.' Karen nodded and watched his face, searching his features for signs of backtracking. There were none.

Her resolve strengthened as she realised that he really meant it. Surely if he understood *why*, the rest of the conversation would be easy.

'I'm sorry, okay?'

She stared at him, waiting for more. *Needing* more.

'It wasn't fair. I didn't think about how it would make you feel. I panicked—' he broke off. Pursed his lips. 'I need to stop letting Mum get to me like that. Especially if it makes you feel less than wanted. I don't want that. I've never wanted that.'

Close, but not quite there.

'Okay.' She patted his hand. 'But that's not all we need to talk about.'

'Don't worry, she won't be back for a while. She rang her last night and I told her to be happy for me or stay away. She didn't like it, but that's her problem, not mine. Or yours.'

Though the interruption irked her, the sentiment brought warmth to Karen's chest. She nodded. 'You were busy last night.'

'You have no idea.'

She eyed the empty box of tissues on the coffee table. 'I think I have some idea. From your messages . . .'

'Can we forget the messages? I'm still trying to say something.'

'I am too. We still need to talk about yesterday.'

'Saying what? I fucked up. I'm sorry I put you in such a shitty position. What more is there to say?'

Karen picked at a knot of fabric on the arm of the sofa. She opened her mouth, but no words would come. Thinking of Cindy and the simple way she explained what she needed to do didn't help. Resolve wavered. Once again she wiped her palms on her jeans. 'I don't know where to start.'

'Then say anything.'

She took a deep breath. 'I want to spend more time with you.'

A huge smile broke out on Dan's face. 'Yeah? That's perfect.'

'What?'

'I was trying to figure out what to do for you and last night I figured it out. I've booked us a holiday. Just you and me.'

The twist made Karen pause. She hesitated, wavering between pleasure and frustration as he missed the point. Again.

'What? When? What about work? I've got research to do.' She clutched the sides of the sofa. 'Why didn't you check first? I'm at uni next week, I can't just run off.' Dan's chuckling only fanned her temper. 'Do you know how much this PhD is costing me? I can't vanish for a week and screw it up.'

'Who said anything about a week?'

'You said—'

'I said "holiday." You assumed how long.'

Shuffling in her seat, Karen twisted her fingers in her lap. 'Fine. How long? And where are we going?'

'Sugar Dust.'

She bolted upright. 'What?'

'You heard.'

'Say it again. I need to hear it again.'

'Sugar Dust, licensed fetish club and themed hotel for adults of an *adventurous nature*.' Dan's smile widened. He puffed out his chest and flicked imaginary fluff off his shoulders. 'I booked it this morning. Two nights, from tonight.'

'For real?'

'Yep.'

Karen squealed. All thoughts of the conversation carefully planned on the drive over, disappeared. She leapt to her feet. Whirled in a tight circle. 'Sugar Dust! We're going to Sugar Dust!'

A leap took her across the room to land in Dan's lap. Grabbing his face with both hands she rained kisses on him. 'How? I thought they were booked for months. This is incredible.'

'I'm glad you're happy, Kaz.'

She grinned, staring deep into the large brown pools of his eyes. She bit her lip. 'Sugar Dust . . . I've always wanted to go, but I have to tell you something first.'

Dan leaned forward and nipped her bottom lip. 'How grateful you are? How pleased? How horny?'

'Yes, but—'

'Why don't you show me?' He ran his hands down her shoulders, cupping her breasts briefly before running his hands over her ribs and down to her hips. Grip tight and just shy of painful, he held her in place while tilting his hips into hers. Still grinning, he nibbled her bottom lip again then slid his lips down the side of her throat. The hot press of his mouth and the flick of his tongue made her groan. She wanted to wait, to push him away and keep talking, but already the details were hazy. He licked a wet path down the side of her throat, teasing the site of last night's bite.

'I've already packed,' he whispered against her throat.

'Really?' A pleasurable jolt shivered over her skin, gathering in her stomach where a tingling sensation billowed out and sank downward. 'What did you pack?' Though she made her voice as neutral as possible, she couldn't quite keep the smile off her lips. A smile that grew wider when Dan next spoke.

'Sugar Dust is a special place. You need *special clothes.*'

'You'll only have them off me as soon as we arrive.'

'Not straight away. I want to look around first. Show you off.' His grip on her hips grew tighter still, digging in with his fingers until Karen could feel his nails through her clothing.

She struggled to remain upright. 'Show me off?'

'It's a big event. Lots of people. Stalls. Demos. You've got to look your best. The dress code for the weekend is fetish.'

'So we're going into Barbie Mode?'

Dan frowned. 'I didn't know you called it that.'

She shrugged.

'Yes, Barbie Mode. I like dressing you. It's one of my favourite parts of having a slave. I choose what she wears.' He leaned closer, filling her field of vision until there was nothing else in the world but the passion in his gaze. 'I choose when she wears it.' His finger traced the side of her face. 'When she doesn't.'

His kiss was slow and deep, the tip of his tongue thrusting into Karen's mouth with such possessive force her toes curled.

Beneath her, Dan became "Dan The Dom" again and the change melted every last shred of resistance left. It left her gasping, yearning, desperate for the whip-crack snap of command in his voice.

It was so much easier to be told want to do. To simply say and do as ordered. No need to think, just be.

Karen had to lick her lips twice before she could speak again. 'What did you pack?'

'I thought you might enjoy some pet play, so ears and collar.'

'Tail too?'

'Oh, yes.'

Her arse clenched in response. She bounced up and down on his lap.

'I also packed two corsets, the purple one and the leather one.'

With great effort, Karen yanked her thoughts back from the fantasy already forming in her mind. She slithered off Dan's lap and took a step back. As the distance between them grew, so did the clarity in her mind.

'Great, but we still need to talk. I haven't finished telling you what I decided last night.'

'Sure, tell me anything you need to, but I want you to wear this.'

Dan crossed to the sofa and leaned over the arm. When he straightened, he held a thick, silver bullet with a cord dangling from one rounded end.

'Dan . . .' More heat flushed Karen's body.

He cleared his throat. 'Who?'

'Sir.' She ground her thighs together and shuddered. 'Please, no. You know I can't concentrate while wearing that thing.'

His gleeful expression said he knew full well. He held it out without saying a word.

Karen took the bullet. Her lips twitched, but the part of her mind able to resist the order had already stepped aside. Karen saw the gleam in Dan's eyes and the quiet expectation that came from his dominant self. He wasn't *asking*, and that, more than anything, spoke to parts of Karen's anatomy that wrested control from her rational head. Even his voice changed and plucked the strings of submission within her as surely as a musician manipulates a violin. She became a tool, ready to be pulled, stroked, and plucked at a moment's notice.

'Now?' she whispered.

'Right now and until we get to Sugar Dust.'

She glanced at the wall clock. 'It's barely midday.'

He raised an eyebrow at her.

'But your mum—'

'What about her?' "Dan The Dom" wavered. 'I don't want to talk about her now. This is about us. You wear that bullet and we'll talk. You can even do some uni work.'

Karen bit her lip.

'Come on. Just open your legs. Slip it in. Remember last time? I kept you on the edge for a whole hour. Quivering.

Begging. Creaming all over my hands. Fucking beautiful. Remember?' "Dan The Dom" snapped back into place and held firm. He shoved a hand down the front of his waistband in a deliberate, provocative display. As his fingers worked, his breathing hitched, and Karen realised he was copying her.

'You were hogtied while I sucked your beautiful tits and whipped your fantastic arse. You exploded afterwards,' he added, still grinning. 'On the sheets. The pillow. My face. Never took you for a squirter, Kaz.'

The memory made her squirm. More shivers rippled over her skin until she could almost feel the ropes about her wrists and ankles once more. 'I'm sorry, Sir.'

'No, it was good. I want to see you do it again. You taste amazing.'

Still gnawing her lip, she plucked the bullet from his hands and unfastened her jeans. She let them fall, stepped free, and pulled the front of her knickers forward.

'Slow down, Kaz. I want to help.' He took it back. 'Arms up, please. And stand near the wall.'

'Dan— Sir—'

'Now.'

The bite in his voice acted like a cattle prod. Karen snapped to attention. Never once breaking eye contact, she lifted her hands and linked them behind her head, backing toward the hallway wall.

'Good girl.'

The praise brought a grin to her lips, and she tilted her hips toward him as he traced one finger over the top of her underwear. She watched him bend, lifting her vest high enough to tongue her belly button on the way. The hot moisture of his tongue travelled down, leaving a wet trail in its wake. She shivered, locked her knees and pressed her hips forward, to invite the touch of his strong, confident hands. Slow, teasing, he tucked his fingers into the waistband and pulled them down. The fabric caught on her backside before sliding to her knees.

'Open.' His voice cracked like a whip, making her jump, just like she might beneath the lash of physical one.

Awareness of every extremity made her lightheaded. The tip of each finger, the end of every toe, each inch of skin buzzing, prickling, tickling beneath the intensity of his gaze.

At once she spread her legs, wide enough to stretch the knickers between her knees and hold them there.

'Very good.' Dan crouched in front of her, bullet still clasped in one hand. His gaze travelled over her exposed pussy, so intense she could almost feel it. 'Wet already? Naughty girl.'

'It's your fault.'

'Is it?' He touched her thigh with the tip of his finger and traced a path that felt very much like his name. The contact made muscles low in her stomach clench.

'You say that like you don't enjoy it.' The finger stroked higher, stopping an agonizing inch away from the curls of dark pubic hair. 'Should I stop?'

The answer was yes, she knew that, but as his finger stroked slow circles on her inner thigh Karen could no longer remember why. 'No.'

'Pardon?'

'No, Sir.'

'Okay then.' The finger pushed up, sliding past her outer lips with no effort at all and sinking into Karen's body as far as the second knuckle.

She grunted, steadied her knees, and took several deep breaths. His calm possession of her body rubbed clean the frustration of moments ago. The anger of the night before. If only he could touch her like this all the time, lay claim to her body with a whispered word, a gesture, a glance. It invigorated her and gave her something that no other part of her life allowed: absolute freedom.

'Karen,' Dan's voice became business like. 'I'm going to stick this bullet in your delicious, wet pussy now. I'm going to leave it there, buzzing away, working you up, until we get to Sugar Dust. You aren't going to touch it. Understand?'

'Yes, Sir.'

'Good girl.' He removed his finger and replaced it with the bullet.

The cold, smooth metal slipped inside with ease. Karen took a second to adjust to the intrusion then clamped her inner muscles around it. She sighed. 'Thank you, Sir.'

The smile she received in return only intensified the gratification.

Dan stood, stroking both hands along her thighs on the way. He left his hands at hip level and leaned in, kissing her, long and deep. 'How's your neck?'

The question caught her off guard, focused as she was on the cool smoothness of the egg. 'Fine, I guess.'

'Oh. Guess I didn't bite hard enough.'

Before she could disagree, he lowered his head to the skin between her neck and shoulder and bit down.

'Oh, God. Fuck.' Karen shook beneath the explosion of pain, her spread-legged stance robbing her of stability. Her hands shifted atop her head and only rigid discipline kept them there.

Sometimes pain was a punishment, a way to pay her back for being cheeky. At other times, like this, the pain ran alongside pleasure and turned simple sensations into a bewildering mix of heightened carnality. His rough fingertips captured her hips, steadying her. Ten points of electric contact against her skin squeezing and digging in deep. When her knees buckled, Karen moaned a little thank you as he held her steady and stretched her neck until her head touched the wall. It opened her body to him, a physical demonstration of her desire to give him everything.

Far too soon Dan released his grip. He licked the sore area then stepped back with a smug grin. Karen flopped against the wall panting. Her thoughts struggled to form, like wading through damp cotton wool.

'Pull your underwear up, Kaz.'

It took several tries to do so, with hands shaking like those of her arthritic grandmother. When done, she touched the side of her throat. 'I only meant it wasn't too sore, Sir.'

He shrugged. 'I know.' One hand slipped into his pocket.

An instant later, Karen felt the dull vibration of the bullet as it sprang to life inside her. A flutter of panic tightened her lungs. 'You're not going to leave that going all day, are you?'

'I might.'

'Fuck, I can't— I can't think. Please.'

'Maybe an hour or two.'

She moaned. No way could she endure an hour of torment, not after that bite. She'd come just from the pressure of anticipation. 'But my transcripts,' she babbled. 'If we're away all weekend I need to do some work.'

Dan's hand twitched in his pocket. The vibrations strengthened. Karen gave up on speaking. It was too hard, too much. Her neck throbbed. Her pussy clenched. One hand drifted toward her underwear.

'Hey!' Dan's voice snapped her back. 'You know the rules.'

'But that's not fair.'

'Life isn't fair.'

'Please! Just let me come once then I can do it. I can handle it then. Just once, please.' The shame of begging meant nothing. Not like this. She revelled in the degradation of it just as much as she savoured the triumphant narrowing of Dan's eyes. He had her and they both knew it.

'No. Now tell me the rules.'

Karen clenched her fists to keep them away from her aching groin. 'No touching. No helping. No coming.'

'Good girl.'

The bullet clicked and became still. The sudden stillness made Karen's legs buckle. She slid to the floor, knees drawn up to her chest. Eventually she managed to look up at Dan's face. 'Thank you, Sir.'

Dan tossed his head, winked, and returned to the sofa and his laptop. Karen watched him for a moment before climbing back into her jeans. As she fastened them, the bullet roared once more, a long, pulsing rhythm that made her groan and twist her hips. 'Screw you,' she yelled.

'Later,' came the amused response.

DAN

As Dan parked the car, a low moan quivered from the passenger side. Karen slumped against her seat belt, eyes closed, forehead sweaty. Though she might have argued, Dan had never seen her more beautiful or more desirable. While the car clicked, rumbled, and cooled he stared at her face and longed to touch her, bury himself inside her in every way possible. Instead, he slapped her thigh hard enough to make her yelp.

'Well done, Kaz. Take it out now.'

She moaned, turning a bleary eye toward him. 'I still don't get to come?'

The pitiful tilt of her downturned lips softened his intended response. 'Not yet.'

'I hate you sometimes.'

'You'll thank me later. Promise.'

Her fingers slipped beneath the shiny hem of her latex dress. He enjoyed the contrast of her dark skin against the white material as she fumbled around. Seconds later, she held up the remote controlled bullet, wet and gleaming. The musky scent of her frustrations filled the car and Dan breathed deep, filling his nostrils with the wonderful smell.

'Put it in there.'

Karen shoved the bullet into the glove compartment and composed herself with slow breaths.

'Better?' he asked.

'I suppose.' Glowering, she clambered from the car and kicked the door shut.

Dan chuckled and when Karen walked around to open his door, the grin grew wider. He stroked her burning cheek with the pad of his thumb. 'Karen,' he murmured. 'My sweet, little Kitten. You'll be okay. Before the night is out you'll get to come.'

She whined. 'But I need it now.'

He peered over his shoulder, casting a sweeping gaze left and right. The chance to further tease his slave presented itself in the form of a deserted car park. How could he resist?

'Now?' he whispered. 'Here? In the street? I can do that.' With deft hands, he gripped her slender shoulders and spun her round. Her back pressed flat against his chest, and he stroked the slippery latex clinging to her skin. First her breasts, squeezing the firm globes before skimming down to the small dent of her bellybutton. He tickled her thighs beneath the hem of her dress. She jumped.

'I could,' he breathed in her ear, 'and no one would think anything of it. Not here. I could hold you against the car.' He did, pushing her hands out to lie flat on the roof. Her cheek touched the metal and he watched the condensation of her breath mingle with the wisps of steam rising from the hot surface. She groaned.

'I could pull off your knickers.' Dan released her hands and teased his way back under the dress. He could feel her thighs trembling. 'Wait, you're not wearing any.'

'You bloody took them!'

'I know.' Dan resisted the urge to check his pocket. He knew they were still there, damp and musky. 'One less barrier.' He flipped the bottom of the dress over Karen's high, round arse and tucked it in around her waist. Both hands stroked her exposed skin, watching the pattern of goose bumps prickling in the cool night air. *So fucking beautiful* . . .

'It would only take a few minutes.' He thrust his hips against her. 'Wouldn't even have to pull my trousers down all the way. A quick fuck.' When he nipped her ear, a low growl rumbled at the back of her throat.

Her instant responsiveness made him aware of a

tightening across the front of his trousers. He resisted the urge to adjust himself; wouldn't do to let the submissive know that she was actually the one in charge.

'You'd love that, wouldn't you? A speedy shag against the side of my car in the middle of a public car park. You're such a dirty girl.'

The loud slap of his hand against her arse cheeks made them both jump. The giddy thrill of power made Dan's head spin. His breathing hitched, and he caught the scent of Karen's arousal on his fingers again. It fired his blood as surely as any over the counter aphrodisiac.

'Do you still need to come? Now?' As his breathed the words into her ear, Dan walked his fingers over the curve of her bottom. Passed the top of her thighs and round the front to cup her pussy. So hot. So wet. He groaned. 'You shaved?'

Karen humped his fingers. 'Of course. It's Sugar Dust.'

'I love it when you're smooth down there. It's so fucking sexy. You missed a bit though.'

'You try catching everything with a shitty lady-razor.'

'Don't worry, it's amazing.' Dan glanced over his shoulder. 'Don't move.'

The lights in the huge exclusive club made pools of yellow light on the tarmac. Though he heard the faint notes of music from within, he heard no voices. Saw no people. Perfect. He dropped to his knees behind Karen and pressed his nose against her backside. He rubbed his cheek against her lower one then nipped the fleshy underside of her arse. She gasped. He did it again. A third time. The fourth bite drew forth a strangled wail as he brought his teeth together and turned his head from side to side.

'You're mine,' he whispered, made bold by her intense responses. 'This mark proves you're mine.'

Karen sounded like she might be having trouble breathing. 'You don't need a mark to prove that.'

He traced his finger along her trembling inner thigh. Thick, slippery wetness coated his fingers, a tangible reminder of the day she'd had. He licked it away. 'You've been so good today. It will be worth it, little Kitten.'

'Yes, Sir.'

'Good. You ready?'

'Always.'

/*

'Name, please?'

Dan gazed at the receptionist as though seeing her for the first time, distantly aware that she'd asked the same question three times. She wore a fishnet shirt under which her breasts were clearly visible. Strategic strips of black and red tape covered her nipples. Her make-up matched: bold red lipstick, black nail varnish and black shadow around her narrowed green eyes. 'Sir? I have other people to serve tonight.'

'Scotney,' he said, glancing down at Karen. She looked at him, shifting on her knees and adjusting her hands which she clasped behind her back. The pose lifted her shoulders and thrust out her chest, making her breasts press against the latex. He could see her erect nipples poking through like pebbles. Fierce longing coursed through Dan's body. He controlled it by pinching his arm and turning back to the glaring receptionist. 'Daniel Scotney and Karen Owusu.'

'At last. Thank you.' The woman returned her attention to the computer screen and stabbed at the keyboard. 'Room 12 is ready for you. Key card.' She shoved a white, plastic rectangle across the desk. 'Ground floor is the main hall and stalls. First floor is the Arena. Group scenes take place in sections A and B of the Arena. Individual scenes in section C only.' She paused long enough to crack her chewing gum. 'Dungeons are downstairs. Obviously.'

'Obviously,' he repeated.

The glare intensified. 'Sir, you already have a companion. All the staff wear uniforms like this. If, for any reason, we find you acting inappropriately we'll ask you to leave.'

Dan lifted his gaze to hers. Through the layers of makeup and beneath the tense expression she couldn't be more than twenty years old. He considered pointing out that she wasn't his type. 'I'm sure I'll be fine.' He retrieved the bags. 'Come, Kitten.'

Karen leapt up and trotted after him, careful to keep two paces behind him at all times, arms still crossed behind her back. When he stepped through the double doors separating reception from the parlour, Dan heard a sharp gasp from Karen which matched his own.

'It looks like Moulin Rouge,' she whispered.

Had his vocabulary contained a better description, he might have argued.

Red walls, the one directly ahead lined with black and white pictures. Some showed landscapes, others still life, but most of the ornate gold frames showed scenes from various BDSM activities. Floggings. Suspensions. Needle play. Wax play. Bondage. One near the bottom photographed a man lying beneath a woman calmly urinating on his face. He stared, winced, and looked away.

An usher in black garb noticed his reaction and paused, grinning. 'We haven't allowed water sports here for twelve years. Pity, a lot of people seem to like it.'

'I don't.' Dan forced a note of calm into his voice that he didn't really feel. Just seeing the image took him back to a small, dark room lined with hooks for whips and canes. A short figure walked around him, trailing the tail end of a flogger down his bare back.

He shuddered.

The man shrugged and spoke again, breaking the spell of the memory. 'Me neither, but to each his own, though, right?'

Nodding, Dan turned aside to continue his inspection. Opposite the main double doors, a wide staircase spiralled up to a mezzanine level. A balcony overlooked the entrance parlour. Back at ground level, arches in the walls to the left and right led to other rooms. The free space on every wall held a tantalizing display of toys and tools. More than the décor, Dan noticed the people. Black, white, brown, pink, old, young, male, female, ambiguous, fat, skinny, tall, short. Not for the first time, he marvelled at the wide array and enjoyed the fact that something so close to his heart remained open to anyone and everyone. Some distance behind him, Karen stood with her mouth open.

'You okay?' He watched her face.

'I had no idea it would be so big.'

'It's the biggest event I've been to.'

'Don't leave me. I don't want to be by myself here.'

'Seriously?' He pulled her against him. 'You're not a nervous person.'

'It's too big— I don't know. Just don't leave me. Please, Dan.'

The use of his name wiped the smile away. A fierce urge to protect her momentarily shouldered his awe to one side. 'I won't. You're mine, remember? No one will touch you unless I say so.'

A fraction of the stiffness left her back and shoulders. 'Thank you.'

'Let's find our room.' He turned, took a step, and collided with a short, chubby woman dressed in a floor length gown of slick black leather. Pale patches of flesh showed through holes cut in around her ribs, stomach, and legs.

The women stumbled in her platform heels and almost fell. Her arms flailed, but the man behind her caught her easily, even with his hands bound. He set her upright and glared through the narrow holes of his leather mask.

'Hey,' she snapped, 'look where you're going, fuckwit.'

That voice . . .

His knees buckled. He saw Karen staring at him, her eyes wide and round with confusion.

It can't be her, he begged silently. *Not here, not now.* Looking away from Karen he angled his gaze down to the source of that voice. *Shit.*

Dan stumbled back a step as his weak knees threatened to dump him on the floor. He locked them straight, fighting to stay standing even as his stomach scrunched up like a Celtic knot. Every hair on his body stood out straight then tried to retreat back into his skin, leaving him shivering and twitchy. He stared at the new woman and shuddered.

Green hair, braided and piled high on her head in thick, intricate swirls. Two slender braids framed her face. A riding crop and leather flog dangled from a loop on her left hip, knocking against her fingernails which were also green and an inch long, filed to a claw-like point. Even her lips glimmered green, a bright Day-Glo shade like a cartoon acid spill. The rest of her face looked ghostly white in comparison.

'Beth?' Though his lips moved, Dan barely recognised his own voice.

'Yes, who—' she stopped and squinted at his face. 'Daniel? Dan, wow!' The woman squealed and launched at him, wrapping her arms around his neck and dotting his face with quick, noisy kisses. He could smell her lipstick and the greasy smears of it all over his cheek and jaw. Every contour of her tiny body radiated heat, pressed against his chest like a human flame. He jerked back. Held her at arm's length. 'Beth, what are you doing here?'

'What do you think?' She cast a careless glance at the tall man standing in her shadow. 'Playing.'

'Right.' A sour taste filled his mouth. He swallowed it back. 'Silly question.'

'What about you? Looking for playmates?'

'No, no, no.' Groping behind him, Dan found Karen's arm and yanked her forward. He ignored her startled yelp and pulled her to his side, curling one arm around her shoulders. 'I'm here with Karen.'

'So *this* is Karen. About time I met you.'

Dan felt his girlfriend stiffen.

'About time?' Karen's voice resembled granite.

'Yes, Dan's told me all about you.'

'Really?'

Dan glanced at Karen. The slight tilt to her head and narrowing of her eyes chilled him right to the marrow. He recognised that look; it didn't belong to a submissive. Beth's feral smile only fed his growing unease. Even after so long free of it, that look called to him on a base, untamed level. Something inside him responded to it, equally wild and visceral.

Dan watched Beth's hands, following the slow brush of her fingers along the leather of her dress. On anybody else it might have been an unconscious gesture, but Dan knew better. Despite himself, his gaze followed the path of her fingers along the tops of her breasts. When her pointy green fingernails moved up, he realised they followed an exposed line of scars extending across her chest and collarbone. The cold filling his bones seeped into his skin.

'He's told me nothing about you.' Karen's voice sizzled through the brief silence.

Beth widened her eyes. 'Honestly? Dan, that's so naughty. Why wouldn't you talk about me?'

He could think of no safe way to answer. Part of him longed to grab Karen by the arm and drag her away, but that seemed worse. Though not by much.

'Karen, I'm Bethany. Call me Beth. Though I suppose you should call me Lady Bee while we're here.' She held out her hand.

Karen ignored it. 'Hi, Bethany.'

Hearing that name on Karen's lips murdered any lingering trace of pleasure Dan felt at being there with her. He stared at the two women, one short, round and pale, the other tall, curvy and dark; the personification of his past meeting his present like a lorry crashing into a cyclist. The resulting devastation could easily be as tragic.

A long pause.

Around them, other visitors to the club moved without noticing the drama unfolding in the middle of the entrance hall. Those who did kept well clear. The silence stretched further.

Dan heard his pulse thudding in his ears and realised that he'd held his breath. But he didn't dare let it go. He looked up, eyeing Beth and the cautious, calculating look in her hard blue eyes. She glanced at him before fixing her attention on Karen. Her gaze wandered over the latex dress, lingering on the positioning of her arms.

'She's your sub, right?' With a smooth flourish, she unhooked the riding crop from her hip and brought it down on her open palm. 'I think your training technique needs work. Want to borrow this for a few minutes?'

The loud crack made Dan jump, and he felt Karen do the same. He released his grip on her shoulders and pushed her farther behind him. 'No, thanks.'

'Sure? I don't mind. I'm all for discipline when needed. It's what we're here for, isn't it, Spanx?'

At the sound of his online name, Dan gritted his teeth.

Don't do that, Beth. I'm not that man any more.

Almost as though she heard his thoughts, Beth laughed, the exaggerated girlie giggle he remembered so well. Several heads turned at the sound of that laughter, many of them nodding appreciatively. Striking, rather than beautiful, with that custom-made dress and boldly coloured hair, Beth made up in presence what she lacked in height. Shoulders thrust back, head held high, she oozed self-assuredness that screamed "dominant."

Instead of holding his breath, Dan now found himself breathing hard through his nose. He opened his mouth then closed it again. Several seconds spent thinking of something safe to say yielded no results. He focused on the man in the gimp mask. 'Who are you?'

'Oh, he won't talk to you. His name is Bones.' Beth laughed again, a sound like glass breaking. 'He's new.'

'Another? You really power through them, don't you?'

'I have a healthy appetite. Bones, come.'

Bones stepped forward with his head lowered. Though he towered over Beth by at least two feet, he might have been invisible for the attention he called to himself. His shoulders curled in and his arms hung loose before him, bound at the wrists with a single length of sparkling chain. Beneath the tight black, thong that made his entire outfit, his hairy legs looked red and sore.

Beth reached up and slapped Bones' face, once on each cheek. The thud of flesh on leather sounded vaguely obscene. She did it again and the second time round, Bones stumbled with a soft grunt. 'Such a good boy. I've had him on the carpet.' Beth glanced at his knees. 'Crawling around my feet where he belongs. Sauna now, I need a break. You can massage my feet, can't you?'

The silent giant nodded. Beth grinned and grabbed one of the man's nipples between her thumb and forefinger. She twisted it until he whimpered. 'He's so good. Very obedient. Does exactly what he's told.'

'That's what good slaves do.' Dan made an extra effort to keep his voice level.

'Ain't that the truth? Show them, Bones.'

Though he might have imagined it, Dan thought he saw the taller man hesitate first. When he did turn, Dan gasped. Karen echoed the sound.

Livid whip weals crisscrossed his back. Tiny droplets of blood beaded on the sweaty skin.

Dan winced and took a deep breath before responding. 'I suppose you're pleased with that?' His own skin prickled with sympathy, a ghost of old agony coursing across his body. He gripped his chest through his shirt. Sweat trickled down his spine.

He remembered standing in the middle of a crowded room, filled with strangers in varied states of undress. He wore a tiny black thong, too small to fully contain his raging erection. His knees ached, rubbed raw from crawling across the unforgiving carpet. Cuffed hands rested on the small of his back. A rubber ball-gag filled his mouth crushing his tongue. A whistling sound cut the air, followed by the sharp snap of a cracking whip. He flinched.

No more, please.

He longed to speak aloud, but the ball-gag stoppered everything, even his safe words. The whip cracked again but this time pain came with it, a white-hot line of agony across the tops of his shoulders. Then another that curled around his bicep and kissed his left nipple. Blood beaded on his chest. He screamed into the rubber ball.

Unaware of his discomfort, Beth stroked the welts on Bones' back. Her fingers trembled. 'Very proud. And we're nowhere near his limit. Have you looked around yet?'

'We just arrived.'

'You must check out the Ball Room. It's busy because of the buffet and the vendors but you'll have fun. Take cash, they have loads of nice toys for sale.' She winked and cracked the riding crop against her palm again. 'I just bought this. We'll break it in later.'

A quiver went through Bones' body. Dan saw the other man shift his position and clench his fists in front of his thong.

'Looks like you're both looking forward to it.'

Beth beamed and turned aside. 'We'll see you later. Come, Bones.' She stalked away, trailed by her mostly naked shadow.

Dan looked at those angry red marks and took a deep breath. He let it out slow and rolled his shoulders but the imagined ache there refused to shift. Glancing back, he found Karen staring at Beth's retreating figure, her eyes narrowed to slits.

'Kaz?'

'Who the hell is she?' she snapped.

'No one,' he blurted, too shaken to find a more credible lie.

'How does she know me when I've not heard a word about her? Another addition to your Library, I suppose?'

'God, no.' The idea alarmed him enough that he forgot to lower his voice.

This time, as the curious faces turned toward him, he turned his back to block them out. Yet his back and shoulders continued to prickle with the intensity of their stares.

Relentless, Karen prodded his chest with the tip of her finger. 'Then who is she?'

'Someone from my past.'

She raised her eyebrows.

'Distant past. She's not important anymore.'

'Does she know that? She leapt all over you like a teenage girlfriend.'

Dan frowned. 'Let's just find our room. Please.' He started walking, towing a reluctant Karen toward the stairs. As he did, one hand resting on the small of her back, he wondered if his mother would be so nostalgic about "the one that got away" if she could see Bethany's new hair colour and racy leather dress.

Dan dropped the bags against the wall and dived on to the four-poster's silky red and black sheets. 'This thing is huge.' He felt the sides. 'And look, chains. Straps. Velcro. Rope.' He touched each item in turn, flitting between them like a child in Santa's workshop. 'They've got everything.'

The occasional gleam of silver complemented deep shades of black and red. The room might have been a suite in a normal hotel but for the pictures hanging from the walls. More scenes from BDSM, beautiful black and white prints of bound women, cringing men, and naked groups of both. Thick hooks screwed into the ceiling also gave it away, as did some of the more subtle details like a bowl of condoms rather than fruits and the welcome brochure featuring a pair of handcuffs on the cover.

Something hard caught his shoe and when he bent to look Dan almost keeled over. 'There's a cage under the bed!'

Standing in the doorway, arms still folded behind her back, Karen watched. Her gaze darted over the room, taking it in with a level of calm that Dan recognised from other play sessions. Underneath it he saw a layer of something else.

'What's wrong?' He stopped riffling through the bowl of condoms to stare at her.

'I don't like that woman. She's rough. Savage. I didn't know people were like that.'

He nodded. A flurry of fear made him grip his stomach. 'There's lots of different styles and intensities across the scene. Some people don't mind blood, or piss, or whatever.' Spying her expression he added, 'We're quite mild compared to some I know.'

'I understand that better than I did an hour ago.'

'Karen.' His breath caught in his throat. He saw her downcast eyes. The trembling bottom lip. Her unease punched him like a hammer to the gut, far worse than her anger back in the parlour.

'Karen, you know I'd never do that to you, right?' He reached toward her.

She wouldn't look up.

'Karen? I wouldn't. Ever.' His voice fell to a whisper. Everything in him coiled tight, twisting in on itself again and again until every second was pain. She had to know. Didn't she trust him?

'I don't know what you think of me, but you have to know that I wouldn't do that. Not to you.'

'But you know her.'

'I used to.' He heard the crack of the whip in his head. Flinched as the barbs slashed across his back and chest.

'You played with her?'

'Yes.'

'When?'

To hide his hesitation, Dan paused long enough to sweep hair from his eyes. 'Before you.'

'How long before, Sir?'

Dan rolled off the bed. Mental alarm bells clanged in his head. 'What's the matter with you?' His forehead ached with the effort to keep from screaming.

'Nothing, Sir.'

'No, I mean that. Exactly that. You've gone all formal and pissy.'

'No, I've not.'

'You have. Tell me.'

Karen's expression hardened and her voice, when it came, hissed like a pot on the hob. She stalked closer, forming fists as she came. 'She acts like you've spoken recently, not "before me." Just admit you want to add her to your Library.'

Relief tangled with bemusement. 'What? No, that's not it.'

'You sure? Your eyes were all over her, with that stupid green hair and tits up to her face. You practically crossed your legs.'

Dan shook his head, massaging his back of his neck with one hand. He knew Karen well, or thought he did, but the yo-yoing nature of this conversation made him weary. 'Is this about the Library? You keep bringing it up.'

'No, it's about her draping all over you like a scarf with tits.'

Dan spoke slowly, hoping to cut off further questions about his past once and for all. 'I'm not interested in Beth. I don't want any other woman but you. You're the one I care for.'

'But you'll still play with slaves from your Library when I'm not around?'

Another switch. He blinked. 'Of course, that's what they're for.'

Karen gasped as though slapped. 'At least I know where I stand now.' She stomped toward the door. She reached it and yanked it open before Dan managed to gather himself. He raced after her, slapping the door shut just before she walked through.

'Move,' she snarled.

Lost and adrift he tried to catch a glimpse of her face. He needed a clue, a sign, a glare, anything. 'Hang on—'

'No!' She clawed at his fingers. 'Get out of my way. I can't look at you right now.'

'What have I done?'

'Just let me go.'

'No, you need to tell me what I did. Fuck— I can't read your mind.' He locked the door and shoved the card key into the front of his trousers. 'What's got your thong in a knot?' His fingers stung where she'd scratched them.

'What do you think?'

'I don't know. That's the point.'

'The Library. The bloody Slave Library.'

He gazed down at her narrowed eyes, twisted lip and furrowed brow. 'You don't like it?'

'Well done, Sherlock. Bright spark, aren't you?'

'Okay, wait a second.' Dan raised his hands, palm out. 'I love my Slave Library, I thought you did too. It's a fantasy come to life, I don't want to give it up.'

'Fuck you, then. Selfish bastard.'

He ducked beneath her flailing arm, hissing when her nails scraped his cheek. 'Karen! Christ, what's wrong with you?' His mouth dried as fear clutched his heart. Never before had she struck him. Not like this. 'Will you listen for a second?'

'I'm done listening.'

'Really? Because it doesn't seem like you've started. You don't get it.'

'You want to pick from a bunch of beautiful women to fuck whenever you want. What's to get?'

Dan's cheek stung as a bead of sweat rolled off his forehead and into the scratches. His tingling skin itched and heat flushed his face and neck. He opened and closed his fingers over his palms, utterly blindsided. 'Is that really what you think?'

'It's the truth.'

'No, I want a bunch of women to pick from so I can have fun with them *with you*.'

'Lucky me, I—'

'Kaz! Shut up and listen to the words I'm saying instead of the ones you *think* you hear.' Frustration made his voice harsh. Loud. He found himself slipping towards that headspace he visited every time they played. But he didn't fight it. He knew she responded to that. 'What happened on Monday?'

'Hannah and Rebecca came over and you screwed the living hell out of us.'

'Did I?'

'Yes.' Her eyes flashed, but her voice levelled off. As he hoped, the change in his voice and stance brought out the same in hers. Karen teetered on the edge of her vanilla self and the submissive who longed to receive and accept orders.

'Becky sucked you off. Hannah sat on my face, then you bent me over the sofa and fucked me senseless.'

'Exactly. *You*. Not Hannah. Not Rebecca. I've never slept with them.'

'They give you blowjobs all the time.'

'But have I ever stuck my cock in their cunts before?'

The vulgar language seemed to penetrate where rational words couldn't.

Karen paused. 'No . . .' Wonder filled that single syllable.

'Right.' Heartened by the break in her attack, Dan ploughed on. 'I like them, I won't deny it. Three beautiful women willing to let me do anything I want to them; why the hell wouldn't I like it? It's a straight man's dream. But I fuck their mouths if I fuck them at all. Only you get the real deal. Understand?' The word came out almost as a demand, but a beseeching undercurrent ran beneath it.

'When I'm done, or bored, I close my Library, send them home, and spend the rest of my time with the only slave I actually give a damn about.'

The bunched fists at Karen's sides loosened. He watched her face, waiting for the next explosion. It never came.

'God, you're right. You've never had proper sex with them. Not once.'

Dan risked stepping away from the door. He lowered his voice, only aware he had been shouting because of the depth of the silence he now broke. 'You're not fussy about playmates. I am. Having men in my Slave Library would kill it. Sorry, I just don't swing that way. But women means that I can enjoy them *with you*. Then they go away and we have each other. That's always what it was.'

'I thought . . .' Karen deflated like a pricked balloon. She stepped away from the door and sat on the end of the bed. 'Shit.'

'Is that what this is about? The whole time? How long have you been thinking this?'

'I don't know.' A weary note crept into her voice. It startled Dan more than the anger or exasperation because it belonged to neither vanilla-Karen nor submissive-Karen. This was wholly new. This was *timid*-Karen. He opened his mouth, but the words stuck. How was he supposed to treat this unknown version of his girlfriend?

'Fuck,' she murmured.

'I don't know how to fix problems if you don't tell me about them. Why didn't you say something sooner? We need to talk about this. We have to—' he broke off, raking a hand through his hair. Relief that Beth wasn't the problem faded as the depth of the real issue started to sink in.

'The Library has been running for weeks. You sat with me when I met Hannah— you liked her. And Rebecca . . . you leapt on her as soon as I let you. Was it all a lie?'

'No.'

'Then why? I don't understand.'

'Normally I don't think about it. But then your mum showed up— you ran away and abandoned me— and she was so awful. But you wouldn't say anything. You never say anything to her. I panicked.'

'Why?' He tilted his head to catch a glimpse of her eyes, but she refused to look his way. Blind without her expression as a guide, Dan forced himself to wait.

Karen bit her lip. 'Because I don't know what you want.' The words burst from her lips. 'I say "I love you" and you just stare like I've punched you. You've never told me you love me. Not once. But you let me meet your parents and your friends and I know that must mean something. You told me you never mix kink with family so I know what we have is different. I visit you and stay for weeks, we pick out furniture together, but if anyone mentions marriage you close up like a clam. You tell people marriage is only for morons who want expensive parties and big dresses.'

'Do *you* want to get married?'

'Fuck, no,' she said, unknowingly aping his response to the same question. 'But what are we doing? Where are we going?'

Dan rubbed his face with both hands. Only then did he realise they were shaking. He made tight fists and held them until the tremors subsided. 'We're a couple. You're my girlfriend, my slave. My submissive. Isn't that what you want?'

'Yes, but I need more.' Finally she looked up. Tears rolled down her face. Words caught in his throat. Never before had he seen Karen cry. His legs jerked as if to run, a classic example of the fight or flight response guiding his body, every muscle ready to move at the smallest provocation.

'Kaz—'

'I'm sorry.' As if sensing the effect of her tears she rubbed the heels of her palms across her face. 'I know you have commitment issues, but you asked. And you're right, you have to know how I feel. This is what I want from you. This is what I need.'

He grasped for a sensible reply. 'I don't have commitment issues.'

She gave him a dry look, one eyebrow quirked up towards her hairline.

Clearly not the right response.

'We've been together eighteen months,' he said. 'That's ages.'

'Dan . . .'

He stared at her. Tracing the lines of her beautiful face and moving his gaze down, drinking in her curvy frame encased in shiny, clinging latex. Once again the contrast stuck him dumb, white against the rich, chocolate brown of her smooth, soft skin. He remembered telling Pete that he didn't want to lose her but only in that moment did he really understand why. It wasn't just her beauty or her submission. Those things certainly helped, but as Dan gazed at Karen's tear streaked face he realised it was the whole bloody package.

From her moisturisers and hair care products claiming all the space in his bathroom, to the honesty she brandished like a blade every time they spoke. The exciting and sometimes ridiculous dinners cobbled together from the food at the back of the fridge. The passion and enthusiasm she brought to her PhD. The surprise gifts of DVDs and chocolate bars after a hard day. The willingness to try new things. The way her soft hands played with the curls of hair on his chest as she drifted to sleep after an intense play session. All of it.

'Wait there,' he whispered.

He opened one of the bags and riffled through the contents. Several coils of rope, soft and coarse, slithered to the ground. Slender lengths of chain went with them, followed by two spreader bars, a ball gag, two vibrators and a fake foxtail attached to a butt plug. Right at the bottom he found what he wanted.

Deep breath.

'I know what you want me to say, and I'm sorry. Those words are so heavy and the last time I said them it was a complete fuck up.' Dan shoved aside the mental image of glossy, green hair and long, pointed fingernails. 'I don't want to do that with you. You're different to anyone I've ever been with. Anyone I've known.'

'I don't know what to say to that, Dan.'

Say you understand, he wanted to scream. Instead he held out a square, purple box tied with silver ribbon.

'Then take this.'

She stared at it.

He shook it. 'Please.'

She did, holding the box in both hands. An age passed before she tugged on the ribbon, unfurling the extravagant bow. Inside, scrunched up purple tissue paper hid the treasures beneath. Her fingers pulled it free, a piece at a time.

Dan watched her, swallowing to douse the taste of bile clawing up his throat. He longed to sit down, but worry that any movement would distract her kept him firmly in place. A little smile touched her mouth. She liked it already. One by one she spread the tissue paper sheets flat over her palm and stacked them on a low dresser. The ribbon she curled on top.

'Karen, you're killing me here.'

'I like presents,' she whispered.

'I know, but open it already.'

She did. Gazed inside. Gasped. 'Oh, Dan.'

A little of the weight on his shoulders began to lift. 'You'll need help putting it on. Can I?'

She nodded.

He closed the distance between them and pulled three silver rings out of the box. With them came a complex arrangement of thin chains studded with glistening white gems.

'Give me your wrist.' He fastened the thickest chain around her left wrist and stretched the last three along the back of her hand. He then pushed the rings attached to each on to her middle fingers. It looked beautiful there, catching the light and sparkling. It dazzled like her smile and in that moment Dan knew he'd done the right thing.

'I found it at the Karnival of Carnal Kink. I can't just say *those words* but I can give you that.'

Karen stroked the intricate piece of jewellery. Her eyes glistened with fresh tears, but these came with a dazzling smile. 'It's beautiful.'

Seeing the slave band on her wrist almost took his breath away. What he didn't add was that he'd found it at the Karnival four months ago and hidden it while gathering the nerve to give it to her. Collaring was no small matter and he wanted to be sure before offering it. He silently scolded himself for waiting so long. The bracelet looked so right against her skin, a physical mark of his ownership of her. His commitment to protect her. And her promise to serve him.

'You know what it is?' he whispered. 'What it means?'

She nodded.

'Do you want it?'

Karen gazed up at his face. The tears coursed down her beautiful cheeks and dripped off the end of her chin. 'Yes, I accept. And I love you too.'

KAREN

'He did what?'

Karen held the phone away from her ear until sure Cindy's last shrieks had faded. 'Collared me.'

'That's a big deal. Isn't it?'

'Yes.' Karen gazed at her bracelet and paused to let her grin subside. When it didn't, she kept talking anyway. 'A very big deal.'

'What's it look like? Is there a big loop at the front so he can drag you around? Does it have studs? Sparkly bits? Spikes?'

'No, you mad woman, it's not an actual collar. That's just the term. He bought me a slave band.'

'A what?'

'A bracelet attached to rings on chains.'

'Oh.' Cindy voice fell. 'I have four of those. I didn't know they were slave bands.'

Karen put the phone on speaker so she could fix her hair. She dragged a comb through it while sneaking gleeful glances at the bracelet. 'It isn't, that's just what we call them.'

'I don't get it. No collar?'

'Collaring isn't about a literal collar, it's about the commitment. Like saying "I'm yours and your mine." It formalises it.'

'That's so . . . cute.' The hitch in Cindy's voice hinted at laughter, quickly suppressed.

Karen ignored it, too high on glee to care much about teasing. 'Dan has a thing for chains, we use them all the time. I saw a bracelet like it in the market last year with a bunch of other fetish jewellery and when I showed him that's just what he called it. The name stuck.'

'You two must live and breathe kink. So do you feel better now?'

The loaded question forced Karen to stop playing with her hair. She stared at her reflection, taking in the sparkling eyes, easy smile and furrow free forehead. 'I feel amazing.'

'And you're going to celebrate by . . . ?'

'Visiting the dungeons.' Another grin captured her lips. She gave a small squeak of excitement.

'Oooooo.' Cindy whistled. 'Because you're a naughty girl?'

'No. I asked to. Later!' Karen blew a huge raspberry and disconnected the call.

In the silence that followed Karen adjusted her skirt to sit low on her hips. The soft, purple leather stopped at mid-thigh with a daring slit up either side revealing bare leg and a flash of arse as she moved. She gave it one last tug then pulled off her bra, which she left beside the small basket filled with condoms and miniature tubes of lube. After a few nervous seconds of assessing her bare breasts, she left the bathroom. She found Dan sitting on the end of the bed. Beside him lay a pair of wrist and ankle cuffs, both in leather. Her favourite collar, again leather, but purple rather than black, with an enormous bell dangling from a loop at the front. He held a simple black headband with a pair of large, furry ears attached.

'Tonight you're my little kitten,' he said.

She nodded. 'Tail?'

'No. You might need to sit. Maybe later. But ears and bell for sure.' He stroked up beneath her skirt. 'Mmm, no knickers. Good. Just checking you hadn't sneaked them back on.'

'I know better.' She spread her legs just enough to allow his fingers to creep up and brush her naked slit.

He grinned, pride and pleasure shining in his eyes. 'Good. Let's get you dressed.'

While it might not have the same significance for other couples, Karen loved the intimacy of "getting dressed." Dan added each piece of clothing himself, careful to stroke, prod, and caress on the way. With the click of every clasp, the tightening of every buckle, Karen felt closer to him and more owned by him.

A little shiver rippled through her as the first leather strap closed over her wrist. It cinched tight and the solid pressure reduced mobility there and made her heart quicken. The leather creaked as he fastened the second one, its faintly woody scent filling her nostrils. Hardening nipples drew her attention downward while the heat in her chest and stomach burst in long, fanning tendrils that flowed through the rest of her body. Dan's hands teased down her legs until they reached her ankles, stroking each one before adding more leather.

'Now the collar,' he whispered.

Karen closed her eyes and tracked Dan's movements with her ears.

Feather light, his fingers whispered over her throat, lingering in the hollow where a faint ache reminded her of the sharp press of his teeth. He kissed her. Traced both her lips with the very tip of his tongue then kissed her again, invading her mouth with an insistent thrust.

Beneath the brush of his stubbly jaw, her skin prickled. He tasted of mint and the scent of toothpaste lingered long after his lips left hers. Fresh sparks of pleasure filled her groin, and she rubbed her thighs together. The bell jangled. Thick leather creaked and a faint whiff of Dan's shower gel filled Karen's nostrils before the collar closed about her throat. She opened her eyes and found Dan watching her. His expression fanned the fire in her belly. She groaned.

'Do we have to go back out there, Sir?'

'No.' Again he traced her lips with his tongue. 'But I want to.'

'Let's stay here.' She touched his hip with one hand, thumbing an erect nipple through his shirt with the other. 'Let me suck you again.'

Grinning, Dan kissed her fingers then stepped back. 'Later, little Kitten.'

Karen sighed. Nodded. 'Yes, Sir.'

'That's my girl.' He moved close again, near enough to touch her nose with his. His eyes were dark and filled with the need she felt in his trembling hand as he cupped her cheek. 'You're so beautiful,' he whispered.

She squirmed beneath his touch. Her cheeks warmed, a softer heat filling her lower body. 'Thanks, Sir.'

He fitted the headband on to her hair. 'Let's go.'

Karen glanced at Dan from her position on the floor. Pressed close to his legs, she could feel the rumble of his voice through her chest. She pawed the carpet and glanced over her shoulder at the milling crowds.

The soft murmur of conversation filled the air, broken occasionally by the crack of a whip, or a surprised shriek from one of the demo stalls. One in particular, with a large crowd jostling for space, demonstrated a selection of violet wand attachments. The scent of ozone and singed hair stung her nose.

Dan stepped forward, peering at a selection of riding crops. The motion tugged the lead attached to her collar, and she shuffled across the soft carpet. A couple of mewling cries didn't catch his attention nor did a gentle "paw" against his foot. So she lowered her head to his ankle and bit him through his trouser leg.

'Ow, what?'

A crop bounced off Karen's head.

'What's wrong?' He bent to rub his ankle.

Swallowing the urge to smirk, she mimed eating from a bowl on the floor.

His expression softened. 'Poor, Kitten. Okay.' He handed some cash to the vendor and retrieved the fallen crop.

The shaft was blue with black stripes and a flat, heart shaped head. He gave it an experimental swish, swatting at her shoulders. 'Very nice. What do you want?'

Karen craned her neck. Then mewled.

'Oh, go on then.'

Both knees creaked in gratitude as she bounded to her feet. When Dan unclipped the lead from her collar she stretched then cast a pointed glance at the buffet table. Another mew.

'Find yourself something nice,' he said, still swishing the crop. 'Bring it back to me.'

Spurred by the growling of her stomach, Karen bounded over to the table and began piling snacks on a plate. She reached the mini sausages and bumped hands with a tall, broad figure wearing a full-head leather mask, thong, and little else.

'Sorry,' he said, muffled by leather.

'It's fine.' She waited for him to move aside but he didn't. Instead, he stepped closer and dropped a heavy hand on her shoulder.

'You're Spanx's kitten.'

Her breathing quickened as she recognised the figure as the one looming over Bethany earlier that night. Bones. She searched the area behind him for his companion.

'It is you, right? Karen?'

She stepped back and brought her plate close to her stomach. 'Yes.'

He made a sound like a purr, though through the leather it sounded more like a growl. 'Pretty little pussy, aren't you?'

Stunned, her mouth opened and closed twice before words came out. When they did, they were soft and strangled. 'Thank you.'

'How long are you staying?'

'Two nights.'

He smiled, or seemed to, through the narrow mouth slit in the mask. 'Same here. We're looking for playmates to pass some of the time. Don't suppose you know anyone?' He touched her shoulder again, this time with the tip of his finger, tracing a lazy swirl down her arm.

Karen jumped. Frowned. Stepped back until her hip bumped the buffet table. 'I—' She fought back the tiny flutter of unease.

He's just trying his luck, like any idiot in a nightclub.

'I only know Master.' She made her voice clear and firm.

Bones glanced past her then back again. This time there was no mistaking the motions of his mouth. A sneer. 'Yes, Spanx. Lady Bee told me about him. A bit soft, isn't he?'

The plate creaked as Karen tightened her grip on it. 'Depends what you mean by soft.'

'A bit vanilla.'

Unease became irritation. 'Everyone has their own style.'

'If you say so.' This time Bones grabbed her arm, a tight, crushing grip. His gaze lingered on her bare breasts. 'Why don't you come with me? Experience *my* style.'

She jerked free. 'You're a sub.' Confusion tightened her lips.

'Only for Lady Bee. I switch quite comfortably when the mood takes me.' He slid forward, close enough that his hip pressed into her side and his long arm draped around her shoulder, pulling her in to his chest.

Karen's stomach lurched. Stiffness crawled across her neck and shoulders. She looked for Dan, but he faced the other way, talking to another vendor selling nipple clamps and matching weights. 'Let go.'

'Come to our table.'

'No.'

'Come on.' White teeth flashed through the gap in the mask. 'Bring Spanx if you must. I'm sure Lady Bee won't mind spanking his arse. Where do you think he got the name?'

She narrowed her eyes. 'Master doesn't sub.'

'That's not what I've heard.'

She sucked her teeth, and took the proffered bait, fighting to control her temper. 'Meaning?'

Instead of answering, Bones steered her around, plate and all. His arm became an immovable weight, inexorably guiding her away from the table, away from the food, and away from Dan.

'Wait—'

'It's fine,' he cut across her. 'We're just going for a walk.'

She heard her heartbeat flood her ears. Felt a hot flush of blood through her veins. Tightening in her throat that had nothing to do with the collar. Thinking of the collar reminded her she was trapped. Locked in the social niceties expected between dominants and submissives. This was nothing like a nightclub.

At a loss, Karen tossed back her head and screeched, high and shrill. The call fell somewhere between harpy and cat's tail stuck in a door, but it had the affect she wanted. Bones grunted and leaned back, taking his rough hands with him.

A hush rippled through the crowd. The whip stopped cracking. Several heads turned in her direction. Two ushers paused their conversation and watched closely, one taking half a step forward.

'What the hell?' Bones looked angry instead of alarmed. His arm snaked out yet again and she opened her mouth to repeat the call.

Then, Dan stood at her side, slapping at Bones' approaching hand. 'Down,' he snapped.

Karen's knees immediately hit the carpet, hands forming fists that she let rest in her lap. The abandoned plate rolled away, leaving a trail of mini sausages, scotch eggs, and grapes.

Just as her own anger began to burn, the comforting warmth of Dan's fingers touched the back of her neck. Sighing, she leaned against his shins and closed her eyes while her heart rate returned to normal. Master would protect her.

'What are you playing at?'

It took several seconds to realise the question wasn't aimed at her. She risked looking up and saw Dan staring at Bones with an expression she had never seen before. Dark. Cold. Angry— no, *livid*.

Bones chuckled. 'Talking to the pussy.'

She hissed at him, falling back into her role easily with Dan at her side. Her nails raked Bones' shin, and he flinched back with a cry.

'Kitten,' Dan corrected. 'And you weren't talking. You were touching.'

Bones rubbed his scratched leg. 'Was I?'

'Yes. It's not allowed without permission.'

'Your permission, I suppose? Big, bad dominant that you are.'

Dan took a single step forward. 'Hers.'

The response seemed to catch Bones off guard. His mouth twitched beneath the mask. 'Hers?'

'Damn right. And if you don't understand why then you shouldn't be here. Come.'

This last part Karen knew was meant for her and she followed Dan on her hands and knees as he stalked away.

Her crawl turned into a lope, then an awkward half gallop as his pace became too much. She cried out.

'Sorry, Kaz. Two legs now.'

She stood just as the ushers arrived.

'Everything, okay?' said the first, a sandy haired man with a body shaped like a bowling pin.

Dan blew a deep breath through his nose. 'Minor misunderstanding. We're fine.'

'Sure?'

'Yes, thanks. I'm taking her downstairs now.'

In any other situation Karen might have resented that conversation about her welfare failed to include her opinion. Here, with her heart still racing, her head still light and dizzy, she could think of nothing more than her narrow escape.

'Fine. Have fun.' The usher beckoned his companion and they moved back into the crowds, aiming for Bones who stared at them with his arms folded.

Karen's stomach writhed. The air felt hot and close, tight in her chest.

'You okay?' Dan's voice caressed her ear, soft and soothing.

'No, Sir.'

'What did he do?'

'Nothing really.' She wrung her hands. 'But I've never felt like that before. Helpless. I didn't know what to do.'

'You don't normally have a problem with idiots like that.'

'I don't normally meet them at kink clubs, Sir. That was new to me. I don't know the protocol.'

Dan stared for so long that she felt her cheeks grow warm. She tried to duck her head, but he tucked his fingers beneath her chin and held her in place. 'Don't look away from me, Kaz. I want you to look at me when I tell you this.'

His tone made her focus on his eyes.

'You're mine, understand? But if another dickhead like that comes along while we're playing, do whatever you need to. Punch him, kick him in the balls, I don't care. But don't make yourself a victim. You're not a victim . . . never have been. That's one of the reasons I love you.'

Karen's heart skipped in her chest. Sounds died away. Crowds faded. Nothing existed but the sincerity of Dan's voice and the firm pressure of his hands on her shoulders. His eyes, brown and intense, fixed on hers as though she were the only other being in the world.

A giggle slipped out of her mouth. Even to her own ears it sounded crazed, but before she could stop it, another one followed. Within an instant she was laughing openly, the wild, hysterical song of one thrilled to the point of bursting. She wanted to sing. To leap into the air. To scream and shout at the top of her lungs, to hug anybody who would let her.

He stared at her. 'What?'

'You said it,' she burst out, stuffing one hand against her mouth, as if that small gesture might stop her glee from spilling over.

'What?'

'You love me. You said you love me.'

'No.' Dan's face turned a queer shade of green. 'I didn't. I said—'

'You did,' she insisted, prodding him in the chest. '"One of the reasons you love me," that's what you said.' With a hop she threw her arms around his neck and hugged him close.

He froze beneath her, but even his stunned silence couldn't temper the joy.

Dan eventually pulled back. 'Okay.' A tide of red crept up his neck and face. A little stutter broke up his words. 'Now what? What does that mean?'

She kissed his nose. 'Nothing. Everything. Don't worry about it.'

He cleared his throat and tugged his shirt collar. 'Let's get something to eat.' Avoiding her eyes, he led her back to the buffet table.

Karen smiled the whole time, gazing at the side of his face while playing with the links of her slave band.

DAN

Dan glanced at the unfamiliar ceiling and sat up straight. Beside him, Karen yelped and slid off the slippery sheets onto the floor face first.

'What the hell?' she snapped, easing back into view. 'You frightened the crap out of me.'

'Sorry. I didn't know where I was for a second.'

Karen rolled her eyes.

'Come up here.'

'I need to pee first.'

He watched her walk away, admiring the play of dappled morning light on her naked skin. Yet again he thought of how lucky he was.

Cat like, he stretched on the bed until his spine and hips cracked. 'How are you feeling?'

'Fine. Why?'

'Not sore? I bloody am.'

A soft snicker came from the bathroom. 'I'm in better shape than you.'

'But you did more acrobatics than me. Where did you learn to bend like that, anyway?'

'Yoga.'

'Really? Hannah can't get her ankles that close to her face, let alone keep them there without her using hands.'

'Hannah clearly doesn't practice enough.'

'Mmm . . . and you question why you're number one in my Library.' He fingered the straps peeping out from beneath the mattress. 'We should get one of these beds.'

'That would go down well with visitors.'

'Why would they be in my room?'

'Your mum?' Karen peered back into the room with a toothbrush clasped in one hand.

'I'm just saying, wouldn't you like one of these?' Unlike usual, mention of his mother failed to fill Dan with slow, creeping dread. As if the events of the night before had shaken her power over him. Grinning, he tugged on one of the massive loops hanging from the rails. 'We could suspend you.'

'We tried once, remember?'

'I'm surprised Pete didn't figure it out then.' Dan thought back to the holes in his living room ceiling.

It seemed such a simple thing; install some hooks, use the recommended knots then hang Karen from the ceiling like a piece of ham. A naked piece of ham, gagged, wet and moaning. She ended up a bruised piece of naked ham, covered in dust and bits of plaster.

Dan smirked. 'I didn't tell *him* how we pulled the fixture down.'

She grunted and returned to cleaning her teeth.

A quick roll out of bed and Dan stretched, scrubbing at his scruffy hair. Something sticky clung to his thigh and he grimaced, peeling a soggy condom off his skin. After tying a knot in the neck he tossed it in the bin and retrieved a fresh pair of boxers from the overnight bag. 'Shall we have breakfast here, or do you want to go back to the Ball Room?'

'Bah ooom.'

'Hurry up then. We over slept.'

Karen's stint in the bathroom was characteristically long. By the time she emerged, freshly scrubbed, moisturised and dressed in tight purple shorts beneath a matching corset, the clock showed 9 a.m. Dan raced through his shower and led the way back to the Ball Room. Before entering, he fastened the purple bell collar around Karen's neck.

Like the night before, the room buzzed with laughter and conversation. In place of stalls and a long buffet table, lots of smaller round tables filled the space, each with six chairs clustered around. Draped with cloths of checked black and red, the tables held racks of toast, platters of eggs, bacon and sausages, bowls for cereal, and large kettles steaming with tea or coffee. Most were full, but Dan eventually settled on a table where two men, dressed in figure hugging dresses sat eating eggs on toast. Both wore wigs, one blond, the other brunet.

'Morning,' said the blond.

'Hi.' Dan pulled out a chair for Karen then sat on the other side, as far away from the two men as he could manage. Despite the distance, his skin prickled.

'Good night?' the stranger continued.

Karen nodded enthusiastically. 'It's so great here. Do you come often?'

The man grinned. He scratched his chin with perfectly manicured nails the colour of claret. 'Is that a pick up?'

Dan opened his mouth to snap "not bloody likely," but Karen got there first.

'No, this is our first time. But you look really comfortable. I'm Karen.'

'I'm Dennis,' said the man. 'This is Henry. Though here, I guess it's safe to say Denise and Henrietta.'

The brunet looked up from his plate and offered a shaky smile.

'I'm Daniel.' He caught a searching look from Karen and ignored it, pouring them both a glass of orange juice.

'Nice to meet you both.' Denise licked a fleck of egg off his fork. Thick hands, with long, calloused fingers tucked a lock of shiny hair behind his ear. 'We do come here a lot. It's a pleasant get-away. Somewhere we can just be ourselves, you know?'

'And the toys don't hurt, right?' Karen laughed.

So did the transvestites.

Dan gritted his teeth and snatched a bowl from the stack. He poured cornflakes into it and added milk. It splashed up the sides and over the table, dripping over the edge and on to his shoes. No one noticed.

Beside him, Karen chatted gaily, occasionally flicking her bell with the back of her hand when she gestured to her slave band or the bite marks on the side of her throat. Jealous of her ease, Dan shovelled food into his mouth and kept his head down. He didn't notice the two new comers until they sat at his side.

'Morning, Spanx!' Beth clapped him on the shoulder.

His spoon flew from his hand and clattered into the bowl. Milk sprayed into his face. He bit back a snarl. No way could this morning get any worse.

'Hi, Beth,' he muttered.

'Vanilla names this morning? Fine, morning, Dan. Paul, say hello.'

The man known previously as Bones tilted his head.

Dan took the time to get a good look at him.

Without the mask, Bones –or Paul – looked deceptively normal. Wide, pale blue eyes, set above a crooked nose with flaring nostrils. White-blond hair, cropped short and an insolent smile that matched the one from last night.

"Sup,' he said.

Instead of answering, Dan looked to Karen. A certain tightness around her mouth and eyes were the only signs of her anger. Dan placed his hand on her knee. His urge to protect her crackled like an electrical surge.

'I'm fine.' She spoke through gritted teeth.

'Paul was telling me how much he enjoyed last night,' Beth announced, as she spread Marmite on a slice of toast. Instead of her ball gown, she wore an under-bust leather corset with a shrug of dark blue lace to cover her breasts, arms, and shoulders. Beneath it, the trail of pale scars was clearly visible. When she saw him looking, her smile grew wider. 'He had fun picking playmates.'

Karen's leg jerked. Dan pressed down on her knee. 'Did he find anybody?'

'Just one girl. Turned out she was a cock-tease though.' Beth sighed. 'I wish I'd seen her; I could have taught her a lesson. Doesn't she know the rules?'

'What rules?' Karen's voice resembled shards of broken glass.

'Don't lead someone on unless you plan to follow through.'

'I don't remember seeing that published anywhere.'

Beth chuckled. She tossed her head and sent her green hair flying in all directions. Henrietta ducked to avoid getting a mouthful. 'Not the Sugar Dust rules, Karen, *The Rules*.' She made air quotes with her fingers. 'The unwritten rules that everyone knows.'

Dan cut a glance at her. He felt a twinge of sadness in realising that she hadn't changed at all. 'What about the rule that says "back the hell off if someone isn't interested"?'

The smaller woman snorted and stabbed at a sausage on her plate with unnecessary force. 'That's just common sense.'

Dan glanced at Paul, pleased to see the other man stare at the table with a pink flush in his cheeks. 'That's right. Nobody wants to give how we live any more bad press. It's hard enough with people assuming rape and domestic abuse. We need to help each other quash that sort of bollocks.'

'Oh, I know!' Denise straightened and gestured with his fork. 'I remember when that book first came out, this place was so busy. Couldn't move for all the wannabes. There was a lot of that then.'

'What?'

'People pushing where they weren't wanted, trying to be *dominant* when in truth they were nothing more than predatory juveniles play-acting at BDSM. As if a bit of kink removes the rules of common decency.' He huffed, flicked his hair, and cut a sympathetic look at Henrietta. 'Some tried to make moves on you, didn't they?'

Dan looked at the two men. His mind struggled to place them together, let alone someone making unwanted moves on Henrietta who was short and dumpy with skin resembling old leather. 'Right.'

He jumped as something struck his shin. A glance to the left revealed Karen, glaring at him.

'What?' he mouthed, rubbing at the sore spot.

'Be nice.'

Sharp responses whirled through his mind, most of them unpleasant. Why should he be nice to these two weirdos? He returned to the safer target presented by Paul. 'You're new to Beth, are you new to the scene too?'

'Yes,' he tore his gaze away from the table top. 'Is it obvious?'

Though he longed to explain that no experienced Dom or sub would pull the stunt he had the night before, Dan couldn't do it. Instead he shrugged. 'A little. But you'll learn soon enough. Some mistakes you only make once. Know what I mean?'

Narrowed eyes and pursed lips were answer enough. Paul rolled his shoulders, and despite his size, seemed smaller than he had a moment ago.

Satisfied, Dan slurped the last of the milk from his cereal bowl and stood. 'I'm going to look around. Coming?'

Karen glanced at him. Then at Denise and Henrietta. 'I'll be along in a bit.'

He blinked, taken aback by her cheery tone. 'I thought you didn't want to be alone.'

'I'll be fine.'

'Don't worry, Daniel, we'll look after her. Won't we, Henrietta?' Denise smiled, his thin lips painted with their delicate lipstick pulled up at the corners.

Henrietta mumbled.

'Really?' Dan focused on Karen. From the corner of his eye he saw Beth lean forward, licking her lips. Fingers of dread crawled down his back. 'We can look at some of the new violet wand attachments or the clamps. You wanted more nipple clamps, right? There are some really nice ones around, we should look at those.'

'In a bit. Unless you want me back in sub mode?' She prepared to stand.

He hesitated. The thought that Karen would rather linger with these strangers than follow him brought an ache to his gut. But showing weakness before Beth resembled waving chocolate in the face of heavy dieters: dangerous and foolhardy.

'No,' he sighed. 'Not in sub mode.'

She grinned. 'Then I'll stick around here. I'll find you later.'

He loitered, searching the room for inspiration, anything to get Karen away from that table.

Beth smiled his way. 'I offered you the crop, Dan. You know what to do.'

'We don't work that way,' he snapped. A stab of anger pierced the despondency coating his insides. 'She can stay if she wants. Later, Kaz.'

'Sure.' She smiled and blew a kiss at him.

A soft derisive chuckle came from Beth's direction. Dan ignored it, knowing that he'd backed himself into a corner by rising to the bait. He mimed catching Karen's kiss then walked away, telling himself that the itch between his shoulder blades had nothing to do with Beth watching him go.

KAREN

Karen smiled at Denise then Henrietta. Their comfortable smiles and obvious closeness brought a warm glow to her chest. She touched the chains running over the back of her hand and felt it again.

'How long have you two been together?'

'Six months.' Once more Denise did the talking. 'Are we that obvious?'

She shrugged. 'There's a vibe about you. Don't worry,' she added at the horrified looks she received in return. 'It's a good thing. I don't see it often enough. Places like this are so much about sex that people forget about the relationship.'

The two men shared a happy glance. On the other side of the table Beth snorted into her coffee. Karen gripped the table, grinding her nails against the wood before angling a hard glare at the other woman. 'What's funny, Bethany?'

'Nothing.'

'Could have fooled me.'

'Your holier-than-thou relationship bullshit. What about the fun?'

'I have plenty of fun. But I'm also here to share something with my boyfriend.'

Beth grinned. 'Bodily fluids and a hot, naked chick?'

'No— yes. Not just that. We're here to share an experience. Because we enjoy giving ourselves to each other.'

'You sound like the back of a Hallmark card. I'm here to spank some dirty bitches who deserve it. The really naughty ones get a taste of this.' She reached to her side and pulled out a whip, which she cracked over the table with a practiced flick of her wrist.

A few soft cheers came from nearby. Paul snickered.

Karen clenched her fists on the tablecloth. 'Then we're here for different things. I doubt we'll have much to say to each other.'

'Oh don't get all prissy.'

'I'm not.'

'No? Practically fanning your petticoats and snorting your smelling salts.'

She took a deep breath. In the still that followed, Karen spotted Henrietta looking at Denise, gnawing his bottom lip. Paul looked delighted and watched everyone with such intensity that he might have been committing the scene to memory.

'I'm not prissy, I'm content. I have something special with Dan and this is one of the ways we express it. When you find something similar you may change your mind.'

'And who says I haven't already? Or that I once did? Bloody presumptuous aren't you? Who says I didn't have it and let it go when I realised what a waste of time it was?' She cast a significant glance at Dan's empty chair.

Karen bolted to her feet. The glasses and bowls leapt across the tablecloth and a small jug of milk wobbled before toppling over. Milk flooded the surface and slipped over the edge. She balled her hands into fists. The very air in her lungs burned on the way out.

Beth smirked.

Fierce tingling raced down her fingernails. They crawled with the need to claw that terrible smile away.

'Bye Denise, bye Henrietta.' She exhaled long and slow. 'I need to find Dan. Sorry we couldn't talk more.'

She strode away without giving them a chance to answer. At the main doors Beth caught up. Though tiny, the other woman showed startling strength and slammed her hand against the wood to hold it shut.

Karen gave a grunt and jerked back. 'Excuse me.' She kept her gaze on the door, while her jaw tightened and her head throbbed with suppressed rage.

'Wait a minute, Karen. I don't know what's got your thong in a knot, but I guess it's something I said.'

This time she did look. Her heart gave a little skip and she became aware of the rush of blood through her body as the familiar phrase struck a chord. She heard it again, in Dan's voice and jerked as if to strike out. At the last moment she pulled her limbs under control.

Heat flushed her face. Muscles across her back and shoulders tensed. 'No shit,' she snapped.

'Let me explain something to you. It might make my attitude easier to understand.' Beth flicked that ridiculous green hair. 'I did the relationship thing. Falling in love. Giving up parts of myself. Living together. It didn't go well. He and I wanted different things.'

Karen frowned. *She can't mean Dan. She just can't.*

'Then it's better that you went your separate ways rather than wasting each other's time.'

'Perhaps. But you should know that *relationships*,' more air quotes, 'aren't always as great as people make out. They can be really one sided.'

'Of course they can, but mine isn't.' The white gems in the slave band caught the light and Karen held it up, unable to stop herself. 'Not that it's any of your business, but he collared me. We're committed now.'

Something dark passed across Beth's eyes. Her upper lip pulled back into a snarl. She traced the delicate links of the bracelet with the end of one claw-like fingernail. 'Christ, you poor deluded, bitch.'

'Excuse me?'

'Do you know how Dan and I met?'

'No. And it doesn't matter.' Though she said it with defiance, Karen felt a twinge of fear.

'Of course it does. Aren't you curious? After last night?'

Of course she was. Her gut writhed with the need to know, but she refused to give Beth the satisfaction of showing it. 'A little, but—'

'What did he say when you asked?'

'You're from his past. Not important.'

Beth chuckled, but not like she was happy. 'Not important. Thanks a bunch, Dan.'

'Just spit it out. I have somewhere to be.'

She folded her arms, making the shrug ride up her breasts. 'Dan and I were a D/s couple.'

'I don't believe you. He wouldn't pair up with . . .'

'Someone like me? You can say it, I don't mind. Just shows you little you know.'

She touched the bracelet again, as if for support. 'He wouldn't.'

'Ask him.' Beth snapped. 'Make him tell you. We were together for two years. We switched occasionally, but I was the sub. It was amazing. *He* was amazing. I thought we'd be together for years.'

When Beth paused, seemingly looking inward, Karen bit her lip. She didn't want to know but she had to. 'And?'

'He collared me five weeks before dumping me for some skinny black bitch he met on *All SCS*.' The blue eyes hardened and swept up and down Karen's body, an obvious display of fury.

Something deep inside roared and lashed out, with the strength of a panther's paw. Far more than the casual racism, Karen reeled at the sense of abandonment and fury pouring off Beth like scalding heat. Cold crawled down Karen's shoulders and sank to fester in her toes.

'He wouldn't do that,' she said.

'No?'

'No, he wouldn't just collar you and leave. He's not cruel.'

'Ask him. He even got me one of those stupid bracelets.' She pointed to the slave band.

Karen leaned against the door; her knees insisted. 'No.'

'Yes. He clipped it on, made a big fuss about it, then bent me over the kitchen sink and fucked me three ways from Sunday. Two months later, he was gone.'

The words fought everything she knew about Dan. His caring nature, his attention, his passion. 'Even if I did believe you, why are you telling me this? Why do you care?'

'Because I can see the signs. You're just like I was. Us girls need to look after each other.'

'Bullshit.' She rallied with a snarl. Stood straight. Jabbed with her finger. 'You're jealous.'

Beth sniffed. 'Even if you are the *All SCS* woman, I don't see much to be jealous of. I'm happy now. Bones is a real catch and even if I don't keep him there are plenty of other arses needing a spank. I don't need Dan.'

Grunting, Karen jerked the door open. 'Stay away from me. Keep your lies to yourself. And keep your pet away from me too. He shouldn't be here.' She walked away without waiting for an answer. Soon she stood in the entrance parlour, gazing sightlessly at the photos lining the walls.

Crowds. Less than the night before, but still busy, bodies in fetish clothing swirling around her like a river current. Voices raised in chatter. Laughter. An occasional happy squeal. The parlour reminded her of a giant playground, but one for kinky grown-ups.

She caught the smell of leather and sweaty bodies, even the faint musk of recent sex from a few who strayed too close. Her fingers itched. She tangled them in her hair, gripping the short strands and pulling. Dan was nowhere in sight, but in that moment, the thought of seeing him only increased her anger. Finally her vision blurred as tears caught on her eyelashes.

'Karen, sweetheart? You okay?'

She looked up. Found kind eyes and a cautious smile. 'Denise?'

'What's wrong?'

'I don't know. I can't—' Verbalising the maelstrom of confusion, anger and fear required strength she no longer possessed. 'Thong in a knot . . . they both said it. What does that mean?'

He reached for her shoulder and squeezed it gently. 'Both? Who? Was it that Beth woman? Did she do something?'

'No. Yes.'

'Which is it?'

'I don't know.' Karen bit her lip. 'She said Dan was—' Frustration boiled within her as the words clung to her tongue. The weight of the slave band threatened to drag her wrist to the floor. When she pressed it to her chest, the warm links dug into her flesh. The pain helped steady her.

'Don't listen to a thing she says. That woman is poison. I knew it the moment she sat down. And that Paul . . . I've seen him before. I'm sure I have.'

'He's new.'

'I never forget a face, sweetheart. I just need to figure out where I've seen him.'

'Thanks Denise, but this isn't helping. I need to find Dan.'

The man gave a kind smile. 'Of course. But first, why don't you come with me and Henrietta for a bit?'

'No.' Steel lined her tone. 'I need to find him. He has some explaining to do.'

Denise raised his hands, palm up. 'It's not my business, sweetheart. But nobody should dive into a delicate conversation when they're this angry. You might say something you don't mean.'

She opened her mouth to argue. Instead, she sighed. 'You're right. But he lied to me. If Beth told the truth, he's lying. If she's messing with me, then she's a fucking bitch and I'm going to—.' Deep breath. 'Dan needs to explain. I don't know what to do.'

'Come with us. Cool off first. We're going to walk around the grounds. I hear there's a really nice St. Andrew's Cross out there.'

'Outside?'

'One must cater for all tastes, sweetheart. Come on. Join us.'

Unlike Paul's entreaties that felt pushy and predatory, Denise's request spoke of nothing but genuine concern. Calm leeched the stiffness from her limbs. She took a deep breath and ran her hands down the sides of her corset. 'Okay. Let's go.'

DAN

The knock at the door made Dan jump. He turned off the TV and swallowed to control his fluttering stomach. *If I can't watch porn here, where the hell else can I watch it?* He continued to grumble as he reached the door and flung it open saying, 'Where have you been? I thought we were going to look at more stalls today.'

Beth raised her eyebrows at him. 'We can look at stalls if you want, Spanx.'

Air jammed in his lungs and lingered there until dizziness fogged his mind. His fingers tightened on the doorframe. 'What are you doing here?'

'I thought we could talk.'

'I can be civil to you in public, but that's it. I've nothing to say to you.'

She chuckled. 'Still upset about the sofa? You got a new one right? That one was ugly anyway.'

The remembered scent of singed faux leather filled his nostrils. 'You nearly burned my flat down. I had to move. The landlord made me pay for smoke damage.'

'That friend of yours is a builder, why couldn't he help?'

'What do you want?' The words oozed through clenched teeth.

'To talk.' She turned her shoulder and barged through, tossing her bag at the bed as she went. A flood of condoms poured out. '. . . And other stuff.'

'Get out.'

'Make me.' Grinning, Beth shucked off her coat. She wore nothing beneath it.

Dan stared. Warmth gathered in his belly and began to travel down. 'I mean it.'

'So do I. You want me out? Come make me.' She stalked toward the bed, bending low to retrieve the bag. She stayed bent over far longer than necessary, wiggling her hips. The motions brought Dan's gaze to the tiny flash of light between her arse cheeks; the green, glittering head of a jewelled butt plug.

'Beth!'

'Yes?' She straightened, brandishing a pair of handcuffs. A quick snap locked her hands together in front of her stomach. 'You used to like cuffing me.'

Dan froze. He stared at Beth, then at the open door. The brightly coloured spill of condoms slid off the bed as she reclined on the silky sheets with her legs crossed.

He kicked the door shut. 'Where's Paul? Or Bones, whatever the hell you called him?'

She shrugged. 'He had to leave. Something about a work deadline.'

'What does he do?'

'No idea. Does it matter? Why do you care?'

'I don't. You want to talk, then talk.'

'Don't you want to come closer?' Beth played with her bright green hair, chewing a small section like a naughty child.

'Talk or get lost.'

'Dan,' Beth cooed. 'Spanx, what happened between us? Why did it end so badly?'

'You tried to burn my flat down.'

'An accident.'

'We both know that's bullshit.'

She smiled and traced her bound hands over the pattern of scars on her chest and shoulders. 'Maybe, but before that. You left. We were so perfect. The terrible things you'd do to me. And what you let me do to you.' Her hands left the scars and gripped her breasts briefly before passing down. She stopped just above the line of her bare pussy and spread her legs, using two fingers to part her outer lips. 'You miss it, don't you? Miss this?'

Even from across the room Dan could smell her. Clear droplets of moisture formed around her fingers and she swirled it around. He jerked his head to the side, but the musky smell of her body lingered. 'Beth, please.'

'Oh, you're asking? I thought you didn't sub anymore.' She snickered. 'Of course you can. Come lick my pussy, Dan. Tongue my clit.'

'You know that's not what I meant.'

'Is that so?' She cast a significant glance at his crotch. 'Fine, I'll suck your cock instead. I won't bite. Unless you want me to.'

He sucked in a sharp breath and angled his hips away from her view. 'Stop it.'

'Why? You used to love it when I sat with my legs like this. Nice and wide. So you could see everything. It's just like before, shaved like you always wanted. Wet like you always wanted.' She fingered herself with more urgency, using her thumb on the base of her clit while thrusting two fingers inside. The damp squelch from between her legs and the hiss of escalated breathing thundered through the sudden silence.

The warmth in Dan's stomach became a burn. Halfway toward the bed he stopped dead, startled that he'd moved at all. His cock struggled for freedom against the confines of his trousers.

'You can't do this,' he whispered. 'Sorry it didn't work out, but it's done. We can't talk about it anymore. I won't.'

Instead of answering, Beth spread her legs even farther and planted her feet on the bed. She raised her hips off the sheets and rolled them in slow circles. 'I'm doing yoga now. And Pilates. You wouldn't believe the way I can bend these days.' She slipped a third finger, inside her body and groaned. A tremor rippled through her body.

'No.' Dan heard the weakness in his voice. He cleared his throat and tried again. 'I need you to leave.'

'Need?'

'I *want* you to leave. Get out before Karen comes back.'

Beth's eyes took on a wicked gleam. Her hair spread across the sheets like an emerald fan. 'Karen. Pretty little Kitten Karen. Where did you find her?'

'None of your business.'

'Was it *All SCS*? The same place you met that other little bitch you dumped me for? Or is she the one? The one you ruined our perfect relationship for?' The fingers slid out of her body with an audible slurping sound. She held them out before her, wet and glistening.

'I didn't dump you for her. I dumped you because you're fucking crazy.'

'I loved you.'

He shook his head. Once upon a time he might have believed it, but after seeing those marks on Paul's back he knew she was incapable. 'You loved what I did to you, it's not the same.'

'You collared me.'

Dan lowered his head. 'I didn't understand what it could mean. I had no idea what it meant to you.'

'You broke my heart.'

That stung but he had nothing to add. Not without opening the doors to a host of emotions he had no strength to handle. Leaving her hadn't been painless. Such a breakup always resulted in multiple casualties. He knew she wouldn't understand that. He looked at the floor again, willing his erection to dissipate so he could think more clearly.

'And now you're going to do the same to Karen.'

Hearing her name from those lips, in that voice, in that tone . . . all sympathy vanished. 'Don't—' he began.

'You gave her one of those stupid bracelets with the rings. And I saw her collar. You're doing it again.'

'No. Don't act like you care about Karen. This is about your ego.'

'You haven't even told her about us, have you? Fucking coward.'

'I love her,' he roared. 'Everything she needs to know she already knows. You need to get over it and move on.'

'You what?'

Dan opened his mouth again, but before he could speak he heard the words again. *Love. Shit. I do love her. I really do.*

'I love her,' he repeated, cold, calm, and slow.

Beth's legs snapped closed. Her eyes blazed. 'Fine.' She rolled off the bed and onto the pile of condoms, treading them flat as she stomped across the room. 'Fine.'

He backed up. 'What are you doing?'

'You need to undo these.' She stretched the handcuff chain. 'The key is in my bag.'

'Then you'll leave?' He searched her eyes, teetering on the edge of believing her.

'Yes. I know when I'm not wanted.'

'Then why did you come?' Edging around her, Dan crossed to the bed and snatched up the bag. 'I can't see it.'

'Near the bottom.'

He dug his hand right in and pawed through the contents. 'No, it isn't.'

'You're still useless.' She rounded the bed. 'Give it. I'll look.' Her enraged searching proved too much for her bound hands. The bag fell and hit the floor near her feet. Dan bent to retrieve it.

Beth lashed out with her foot, catching him in the chin with such force that he cried out. The blow cracked his teeth together and sent him reeling, sprawling against the floor on his back. Stars of gold and purple danced across his vision. Pain spiralled out from his jaw. Before he could move or cry out, Beth dived on to his chest and sat down, pinning his arms with her knees.

'We're not done.' She hissed.

Dan tasted the metallic tang of blood in his mouth. He probed his lips with the end of his tongue and found the small cut from his front teeth. 'Fuck.' Speaking brought on a wave of dizziness. He swallowed and tried again. 'Get off me!'

Instead of standing, she crawled up his body. Dan realised her intent seconds before her musky wetness struck his chin. He tossed his head to one side. Dizziness intensified and made the room spin, while the scent of her body, so wet and ready, made his cock leap to attention. Her nearness, mingled with the savage ache in his mouth took him back to a place so familiar that he groaned. His hips bucked.

Grinning, Beth sat on his mouth. The taste of her brought memories of dungeons and whips, floggers and vibrators, chains and blood. He moaned and wrenched his hands free, gripping her hips as pulsing need fired through his cock.

'Yes,' she whispered, 'just like before. Lick me, Dan. Eat me.'

'No.' More pain. Blood on his lips. Stiffness in his injured jaw. 'I'm not doing this.'

She hissed and ground her pussy harder against his face. 'Keep talking. It feels good, Dan. So good. Just like it used to be.'

'Fuck's sake, Beth!'

Dan heard the click of the door and twisted his head to one side. He froze, hands still locked on Beth's hips when he spotted Karen standing in the doorway.

KAREN

Karen froze outside the room, her pulse thudding in the back of her throat. Her mouth grew dry, though a lingering taste of something hard and bitter lined her tongue. She heard sounds behind her, low voices, but they were white noise, faint buzzing that filled her ears, while mist seemed to crawl across her vision. Then a soft chuckle pulled her back to the present.

Beth leered at her from beneath a curtain of long, green hair. 'Oops.'

Karen looked past her to Dan, searching for his face beneath Beth's long, pale legs. 'Dan?' Her voice came out smaller than she wanted.

'Karen. Let me explain. I know what this looks like, but that's not what it is.'

'Really?'

'Yes. Let me— will you get off me woman!'

Beth laughed, but she did as she was told. 'Of course. I'm only here to do as you ask, Master.'

Hearing another woman call Dan "Master" sickened Karen to the very core. Hearing Beth use the title veiled her vision in deep, pulsing crimson. Adrenaline flushed her limbs and set each one tingling while a rhythmic pounding threatened to drown out all other sounds. She saw the familiar way Dan's hands lingered on those pale, round hips.

His lips and chin glistened to match Beth's inner thighs. Then Beth rolled free, sliding along Dan's chin and chest. In her wake a shining trail of juice stained Dan's shirt. Karen took a step forward and saw the gleam of handcuffs around those tiny wrists.

Denise touched her shoulder. She jumped, having forgotten, he was there. 'Do you want to come with us, again, sweetheart? This looks like a bad time.'

Karen watched Dan struggle to his feet. He flexed his jaw and wiped a slick of Beth's sex-juice from his stubble. She gritted her teeth but her hands shook. 'Yes, please.'

She didn't look at Denise, but kept her gaze on the man she loved.

'Kaz, no. Wait.'

'No!' she roared.

His voice was almost "Dan The Dom," almost commanding. As always, it filled her body with lust and longing, but those feelings couldn't compete with white-hot fury. The quickening of desire melted away, replaced by a yearning to scratch at his eyes.

Karen tore the slave band from her wrist and hurled it to the floor. It hit the carpet with a thump far louder than the delicate piece of jewellery warranted. It was the sound of all her hopes and dreams of a future with this man hitting the dust.

'Don't you dare tell me "no" like you have any right. You've lost that right— no, that *privilege*.'

'Please listen—'

'So you can tell me more half-truths and bald face lies?'

Dan stopped dead. 'What lies?'

'You told me you've never subbed. Explicitly. But she says you did with her. First I thought she was lying but this . . .' Her throat tightened so much that words stopped flowing.

He whirled away to face Beth. 'What did you tell her?'

The smile vanished from the smaller woman's lips. She backed toward the bed. 'The truth.' Beth's face contorted, an ugly expression of fury, and she pointed with her chained hands. 'I told her what we meant to each other and how you threw it away. Like you're probably planning to do with her.'

Karen folded her arms. More than pain, she heard the acidic edge of jealousy in Beth's voice. It pleased her, a wicked spike of vindictive glee.

A short silence followed, filled only with the sound of tense breathing. Then Dan bent and scooped a pile of condoms into a small green bag.

'I'm not going to tell you again, Beth. Get out. You've done enough damage to last forever.'

'But my cuffs—'

'Out!' Dan threw the bag. 'Out!' It hit her in the face. 'Get out before you leave on your arse.'

Beth turned to flee but Karen stepped in to block the way out. She stared into that mean, ugly face and bunched her hands into fists. It would feel so good to hit her, to feel her knuckles grind into that sharp, square jaw. Hear bone crack. A shriek of pain.

In that moment Karen understood why Cindy always aimed for the nads; dealing pain seemed such a quick way to ease her own.

A gentle hand dropped on to her shoulder. Karen turned to see Denise shaking his head. 'Don't.' His voice soothed, pitched low and serene.

Her hands itched.

'She's not worth it, sweetheart. Please don't. You'll get thrown out. They might even call the police.'

The rage dropped to a gentle simmer.

'They could even ban you,' Denise continued. 'You'll never be able to come back. Is that what you want?'

Who the hell would I come here with if not Dan? Karen gnawed her bottom lip. *But she's not worth a criminal record.* Karen stepped to one side. Head high, unconcerned by her nudity, Beth walked past her. On reaching the hallway she stopped and turned. 'He doesn't know what a collar really is, Karen. He'll hurt you.'

A hysterical laugh burbled from her lips. 'As if you give a shit, you two-faced, banshee-haired bitch.' The stunned stare she received in return more than made up for the satisfaction lost from staying her fists. It also reminded her of why Cindy was the one to lash out, and she wasn't.

'Get out of here,' she muttered.

'He doesn't understand what it means to girls like us—'

'Don't you dare couple yourself with me. There's no "us," just you, bringing cretins like Bones into what was once a safe environment, and me forced to deal with the fallout of your neurotic, egocentric, anti-commitment bullshit. Now, fuck off.'

Silence. From the corner of her eye Karen thought she saw Dan smile. With effort she tamped down the pride swelling her chest and focused on the other woman. Beth shook her head. Flicked her hair. Walked away.

Denise held out his hand. 'Come with us, sweetheart. We'll look after you.'

'Get your hairy paws off my girlfriend.' Dan stepped forward. 'She's not going with you.'

A look of horror crossed Denise's face. Karen forced herself between them and gave Dan the full weight of her gaze. 'Arsehole. I knew you had a problem with them from the second we sat down. At least they don't pretend to be anything other than what they are.'

'What's that supposed to mean?'

She rolled her eyes, no longer surprised at his willingness to remain blind to his prejudices. 'It doesn't matter. Come on guys, let's go.' She turned. Denise put his arm around her shoulders. Henrietta grabbed her hand and squeezed it. They led her back along the corridor.

'Karen, please.'

She didn't turn. Not even when Dan's pounding footsteps chased after her. His hand touched her arm as if to pull her back and she jerked away from all three men. 'What?' she cried, horrified to hear the threat of tears in her voice. She sniffed to keep them at bay.

With Beth gone, her anger lost all focus. It transformed into cold, creeping anguish that sapped her strength and left her knees weak.

'Aren't you going to let me explain?'

'I don't see the point.'

'The point?' He clutched great fistfuls of hair with both hands. 'The point is that I love you. Doesn't that deserve a chance?'

The words, so incredible mere hours ago, bounced off her like drops of rain. They didn't— couldn't penetrate. She felt hollow.

She looked at Denise.

'Well if you ask me—' he began.

'I didn't ask you, *Dennis*. Get your greasy, pointed nose out of my face and let me talk to my girlfriend.'

Karen sighed. 'Dan—'

Again he interrupted. 'No! Look, Karen, there's things I've not told you about my past relationships because I was scared or ashamed. Maybe both. I'm not proud of some of the things I've done and I wasn't ready to share that with you. I couldn't stand the thought of you thinking less of me.'

Karen rolled her eyes. She looked at Dan's flushed face and the traces of a dying boner at the front of his trousers. 'Well that went well, didn't it?'

He flinched. 'I deserved that, but it's true. And now I've got nothing left to lose.'

She tried to think of something sensible to say, or at least something meaningful, but the threat of tears clogged the back of her throat and made speaking all but impossible. She shook her head.

'I know this is bad. I know I've fucked up – again – but please hear me out. That's all I'm asking. Let me tell you everything.'

Once more Karen looked to Denise, but this time to gently pat his arm. 'It's okay. I'm sorry he's being such a prick. He's always been uncomfortable around transvestites.'

'Lots of men are, sweetheart.'

'It's no excuse to be rude. He's going to apologise when we're done.'

'There's no need for that.' A look of mild embarrassment crossed Denise's face.

'Yes, there is,' she said. 'I'll come to your room later.'

Denise nodded. With a last look at Dan, he tucked his arm around Henrietta's shoulder and steered them both away.

Karen tilted her chin and stared Dan straight in the eye. She saw him lower his shoulders. 'Ten minutes,' she told him.

'I was new. I didn't really get it.' Dan sat on the end of the bed with his head in his hands. He talked to the floor. 'I knew I wanted to control women. I knew I liked the power trip and that it was important to me sexually. There were no words for it, but I understood that much about why other relationships I'd had didn't work. Finding the BDSM scene introduced me to ideas I'd never considered before and suddenly there were websites full of women who wanted what I did. When Beth came along she was so fiery and pretty and sexy and obedient. She'd do anything I told her.'

Karen glared, thinking back to Beth's bright green hair and nails. 'Is this supposed to help? I want to know how she ended up sitting on your face.'

'You need to understand. I don't know how else to explain other than to start at the beginning.'

'You've got eight minutes.' She glanced at the wall clock to emphasise the point.

He dragged his fingers through his hair. 'I wanted to learn more, and munches were a waste of time, so I went to clubs. I met different people and explored different styles. We even tried it the other way.'

Karen winced. 'Then she didn't lie.'

'What?'

'She told me you switched. I didn't believe her. I'm such an idiot.'

Dan sighed. 'You're not an idiot. Why *would* you believe her?'

'Why, indeed?' She gave a soft, disparaging chuckle.

'I liked switching at first. She used clamps. Light impact. Candle wax. Food. Ropes. Then she talked about water sports. Needles. Cock plugs.'

Karen flinched. 'You hate that stuff.'

'I know.'

She looked at Dan's lowered head and felt a sudden need to touch him. Her hands fluttered as if to reach out, but she jerked them back at the last moment. 'I didn't know. You never told me you'd tried it.'

'How would I know what I liked if it didn't try? Anyway, what was the point? You already *knew* you didn't like that stuff. But Beth ignored my safe words and I ended up with an infection that laid me out for two weeks.'

'How did you end up with someone like that? Why did you stay?'

'She got carried away.'

'You believe that?' Karen gazed at him, seeing and hearing through him the voices of hundreds if not thousands of domestic abuse victims.

'Sometimes. Then I think about it some more and . . .' He scratched the back of his neck. 'It takes a lot of control to control someone and keep a grip on that power trip. It's a big rush. She needed practice. But after that night I only switched in clubs with other people around.'

'You were scared.'

'I suppose.'

'You were scared and still you stayed. You're a fucking idiot.' Irritation tiptoed back into her tone.

Dan nodded in miserable resignation. 'There was one guy who called himself The Big D. He liked to really hurt women. Beth idolised him. She told me that if I wanted to be a "proper Dom," I should take some tips from him about how to treat subs and slaves.'

The next pause lasted longer than Karen expected. 'And?'

'I hurt her.'

'So?'

'No, I *really* hurt her.' Dan didn't look away from the floor, but his shoulders trembled. He gripped his knees until the knuckles turned white. 'I had her tied over a bed. Ropes. She had a ball gag. She wanted me to whip her.'

Watching him shake like that, Karen realised that she wasn't ready to hear this story. Her own body chilled. Her mind raced through different ways to make him stop talking but words refused to leave her mouth.

'I couldn't hear her use the safe word, if she did at all. I have no idea. But she didn't signal me either. She let me keep whipping her. I didn't know what I was doing, nothing about danger zones or soft spots, I just hit her over and over.'

Nausea boiled through her stomach. She pressed one hand to her midriff. 'Dan—'

'She passed out. I didn't realise. Some other guy had to tell me she wasn't moving and then it took half an hour to wake her up.'

Karen bit her lip until it bled. Silence filled the room.

In the distance, as though from another world, voices of other visitors to the club floated through the walls. In one of the rooms nearby a woman screamed in accompaniment to loud, rhythmic pounding against the walls.

Dan took a deep breath. 'We woke her up. I apologised. But she laughed. Said it was the best time of her life. She told me she'd never been so wet or so horny in her life and that the whole thing was perfect. But later that night I saw the marks. She's still got scars, did you see? *I* did that. That was me.'

Karen thought back to the crisscrossing network of raised scars on Beth's shoulders and chest. Her knees wobbled and she leaned against the wall. 'Shit.'

'It was awful. I kept trying to say sorry, but she *liked* it. She loved the idea that I'd marked her forever. She wanted me to do it again in a place where the scars would be visible for everyone to see.'

Though she hated to ask, Karen knew she had to. 'Did you?'

'No.'

She waited, hiding a slow exhalation of relief behind one raised hand.

'I couldn't touch her at all after that. She wanted me to be someone else – like The Big D. But I couldn't. I'm not that person. I'm not . . .'

'You use whips with me,' she whispered. 'We do impact play all the time.'

'Not like that. And I take precautions now. Why do you think I love chains so much?'

She shrugged, wrapping both arms tight around her body.

'I can *hear* them. They make a sound every time you move. So I *know* you're able to communicate if you need to. A safe word or a hand gesture. I don't really want to hurt you. And you don't really want to be hurt. What we do is completely different to anything I saw or did while with Beth.'

Karen hunched down into her shoulders, reaching for her ears as if to block out Dan's words. 'But you collared her.'

'Before I understood what it meant.'

'You got her a slave band.' She pointed to her own bracelet, lying on the floor where she'd thrown it.

'No.' A little of the fire returned to his voice. 'I bought her a pretty piece of jewellery. It's not the same thing.'

'She saw mine and made a big deal of it.'

'Of course she did.' Dan sounded bitter. 'But the slave band thing is me and you. No one else has ever had one like it – not the way I offered it. When I collared Beth, I actually bought her a collar. A big leather brute with a ring on the front. I told her she had to wear it all the time because she was mine. And she did. It's what she wanted. She was the type of woman who didn't feel safe or whole without a Dom around. Male, female, it didn't matter, so long as she had someone to tell her what to do 24/7.'

'Some couples do that.'

'I know. Fred and Georgie are 24/7. But me? I need a woman to fight me every now and then. Or straight up tell me when I'm being an arsehole. I like kink, but it's not my whole life. I need someone I can take to my work's Christmas lunch. Go to the movies with. Introduce to my family without frightening my dad or terrorising my mother.'

Despite herself, Karen smiled. 'So what happened?'

'I panicked and bailed. I'm not proud of it, but I didn't know what else to do.'

Karen sat on the floor. She pressed her hands against her eyes and leaned the back of her head against the door. 'How could you keep all that from me?'

'Shame? Fear?'

'Yesterday, when we met Beth in the foyer, you told me she wasn't important.'

'She's not part of my life anymore. She isn't important, but our history is. You're right. I should have told you.'

'Damn right you should have.' Though the words were harsh, the tone softened with each passing syllable. 'You can't keep things like that from me. It's not fair.'

'Like you and the Slave Library?' His calm voice and steady gaze dampened some of her righteous fire.

'That's not the same.'

'Yes, it is. I didn't tell you about Beth. You didn't tell me how much you hated the Library. If our dynamic is going to work, we both need to be honest with each other. Otherwise it falls apart. I should know.'

Karen searched her mind for something to say but nothing seemed appropriate. Instead she gazed at the floor and replayed all the times she'd thought something and kept it to herself. All the times she'd resented Hannah or Rebecca slurping at his cock while she watched.

God, I'm such a fucking hypocrite.

Shame coiled in her stomach and refused to budge. At last, Dan stood and began to gather their clothes and toys, separating everything into two obvious piles.

She frowned. 'What are you doing?'

'Packing. I'll take you back to your flat. Or anywhere else you want.'

Karen watched him fold clothes and remembered the feel of his powerful fingers skimming over her skin. She watched the tight, stiffness of his shoulders and the jerky motions as he stuffed everything into bags.

She walked toward him. 'Stop, please.'

'Why?' He balled an odd pair of socks and tossed them on top of a shirt.

'I don't want to leave.'

He dropped a pair of jeans and spun to face her. His hands trembled over her shoulders as if afraid to touch. Hope leapt into his eyes. 'Really?'

In answer, she put her hands over his and pushed them down to rest on her shoulders. 'I've not forgiven you yet. And we've got a lot to talk about. But I'm not leaving.'

'Karen.' He tightened his fingers on her skin. 'I'm so sorry.'

'Forget all that now. Just answer one question for me.'

'Sure. Anything.'

She took a deep breath and blurted the words before she could change her mind. 'Do you want to live with me?'

He froze.

'Not me visiting your house, not you visiting my flat once in a blue moon. Do you want to live with me in a house that we've bought and jointly own?'

Dan's lips smacked closed. He stared for several seconds before looking down at the floor. His hands slid away.

Karen felt the loss of his touch as keenly as a loss of air. She gasped and turned aside. Tears gathered in her eyes and she brushed them away with both hands. A sinking feeling in her stomach made her want to drop through the floor, but she locked her knees and held firm. 'Right. It's okay. I just wanted to be sure.'

'Karen?'

'What, Dan? What more can you possibly say?'

'I'll live with you.'

She whirled round. One half of her mind insisted she'd misheard. That after everything else that had happened, desperation to hear something good had muddied her understanding. The other half of her shrieked in delight. 'What?'

Dan smiled, one hand plucking at his sleeve. He dropped his gaze to her toes. 'Yes, I want to live with you. I can't think of anything better.'

She bent to catch his gaze. 'Seriously?'

'Don't make me think about it too much, I'm shitting myself as it is.'

Karen laughed. She couldn't help it. The sound burst from her lips, loud and full, shaking her body from head to foot. She rushed forward and threw her arms around his neck, crushing her body against his.

He held her, turning his face to rest his cheek on her shoulder. 'Just let me break it to Mum, okay?'

Another laugh. 'Sure, Dan. Whatever you want.'

DAN

Dan looked down at his hand. Karen's fingers threaded through his and squeezed. He grinned, raised them to his lips and kissed them. 'Okay,' he muttered, shoving back his nerves. 'Do it. Before I change my mind.'

Karen raised her free hand and rapped her knuckles against the door. He caught the sound of heavy feet approaching. The door opened.

'Hi, Denise.' Karen beamed. 'I told you I'd be back.'

Dan flinched as the older man's gaze swept over him. He shook himself and made the effort to meet those narrowed, grey eyes.

They assessed him then swept sideways to Karen. 'You okay, sweetheart?'

'Fine.'

'And him?' He pointed with one polished fingernail. 'What's he doing here?'

A frown furrowed Dan's brow. He recognised the tension and fought to get rid of it.

Karen squeezed his hand again. 'Dan has something he'd like to say.'

'Does he, now?'

'You have every right to be pissed off,' Dan said at once. 'And every right to make it hard for me. No, I meant difficult— *difficult* for me.' Avoiding Karen's eye, straining to ignore her giggles, he pressed on. 'She's right. I *was* a prick. I have my own prejudices to sort out, but that doesn't mean I have to be a complete arsehat.'

'That's a good start.' Denise crossed his arms. 'Carry on.'

'What you want to wear and what you to call yourself is none of my business. You're not hurting anyone. I shouldn't have said what I said.'

'What about the rest?'

Dan shuffled his feet. 'Sorry, I really don't remember—'

'That stuff you said about my nose. Do you have any idea how much powder I use to keep the shine off?'

Karen snorted. Dan glanced at her, then back to Denise. The transvestite had his eyes scrunched closed and two fingers crammed into his mouth, as if that might hold back his laughter. His shoulders bucked with the effort.

'Really?' Dan sighed. *'That's* funny? I'm really trying.'

'I know, I'm sorry,' Denise reached out with one massive hand and clapped him on the shoulder. 'But you looked so cute standing there with your begging cap in hand. I couldn't resist. Apology accepted. Frankly, I've heard worse in my time but it's big of you to come here and say it. Do you want to come inside for a bit? We have tea.'

'Thanks, but no. We've got some chatting to do.'

'We're moving in together,' Karen burst out, eyes shining.

Her obvious glee made the butterflies in Dan's stomach all worthwhile.

'Really? That's great, sweetheart.' Genuine pleasure filled Denise's features. 'I'm glad Beth hasn't done any lasting damage.'

'Not to us.' Dan took a moment to be grateful for that fact. 'Though she damn near broke my jaw.'

'People like her have no idea what it's all about. It's not just sex and toys, is it Henrietta?'

A muffled grunt came from within the room. Denise leaned forward and whispered behind his hand. 'I've got him in the bed straps with a bridle gag. And a vibrator.'

Dan frowned. 'Where does he put— oh!' He fanned his shirt against his chest and fought the urge to back against the wall. 'Didn't mean to interrupt.'

'No, it's fine. Want to see?'

The very thought filled Dan with dread. 'No, thanks.'

'Yes, please.' Karen spoke at the same moment he did.

He looked at her. 'Really?'

'It will be fun.'

'You think so?'

'Sure. Aren't you curious?' She stroked his arm.

'No. Yes. A little. I don't want to intrude.'

Denise shrugged. 'It's just some fun. And an audience works well, he gets off on it.'

'Don't you want to see?' Eyes shining, Karen stared up at him.

'I'm not sure, Kaz.' Dan looked past her, finding temporary refuge in studying the wallpaper patterns.

'I am.'

Dan stared at her. He took in the wide eyes and toothy grin. 'I don't know if I can.'

Denise backed away. 'Don't force him, sweetheart. If he's not comfortable, no problem. Just thought I'd offer. You both seem nice enough. Henrietta certainly likes you; he'd enjoy having you there. Trust me, that sort of thing tips him right over the edge.'

'Please, Dan?' Karen touched his arm and her pleading expression, coupled with the begging in her voice made the decision for him.

He sighed and worked to fight off the uncomfortable sensation of weight on his chest. 'Okay. For you.'

'Thanks, Dan.'

Denise flung open the door. The room, exactly the same as Dan's, was littered with toys and tools. Some he recognised, others he didn't. In the middle of it, at the end of bed, stood Henrietta. He wore a white t-shirt, stretched taut over his round stomach. Two red clamps gripped his nipples through the fabric. Long black straps secured his arms above his head, stretched out to the tops of the posts. His feet, secured with a spreader bar at its maximum length, rested on the floor. He wore nothing else. Low buzzing filled the room.

Dan stared at the floor and tried to steady his breathing. When he next looked up, he skipped the other man's body to look directly into his eyes. 'Hi.'

Henrietta glanced at him, eyes glazed, skin sweaty with the battle to maintain control. He nodded once and made a soft sound behind the bar of the bridle gag pressed against his teeth.

'Fifteen minutes so far,' said Denise. His chest swelled. 'He's done very well. Barely a peep. Even when I used that.' He pointed at an object on the floor near the TV.

Dan glanced in the direction of his finger, grateful for something else to focus on. 'I've never seen one of those before.' He studied the small metal wheel dotted with spikes.

Karen's eyes lit up. 'A pinwheel. I love those things.'

'Here, sweetheart. Give it a try.'

'Can I?'

The enthusiastic gleam in Karen's eyes made Dan's stomach clench. 'You want to? I didn't know you had any sort of . . .' He flapped his hand as he searched for the right word. 'Domineering tendencies.'

'It's never come up. You don't sub.'

'Right.'

She stared at him. Her shoulders slumped. 'Dan, I'm so sorry. You really don't want to be here, do you?'

He shrugged, simultaneously relieved at her perception and disappointed in his inability to be subtle.

'We just talked about this. We need to be honest with each other. Trust each other. I won't get upset because there's something you don't like.'

'But you were so keen.'

'So? That's me.' She moved closer. 'Dan, I love *you*. I don't want to make you uncomfortable. Let's go.'

'Wait,' he clutched her arm as she aimed for the door.

'You don't have to, Dan. Honestly.'

'I know, but I want to see.'

She frowned.

'I know, but you look so keen. And that's a bit of a turn-on.' As soon as the words left his mouth, Dan's shoulders lifted. His body no longer weighed down on his knees to the point of discomfort.

'Really? You're not just saying that?'

'Positive. Go on. Do whatever it is you planned to do.'

Karen bounded across the room and dropped to a kneeling position beside Henrietta. She held out one hand and Denise lowered the pinwheel into it. Her slender fingers touched Henrietta's bare thigh, gliding up then down.

Dan frowned before he could stop himself.

Denise cleared his throat. 'Relax, Dan. I don't think he's her type.'

'What?'

He cast a significant glance at Karen. 'I *know* she's not his type. You're safe.'

'I didn't say anything,' he said huffily.

'Your body did. And now you're blushing.' He rubbed the side of his nose. 'It seems to me that Karen has an itch she needs to scratch. And you just told her to. She did ask, remember? This is a safe place for her explore since neither I nor Henrietta are competition. After this, if you want, you can talk to her about it.' He shrugged. 'But if she's still with you after all that drama with Beth then a little fun with a pinwheel isn't going to change anything.'

Dan gazed at the other man and felt a grudging flicker of respect. 'Pretty sharp, aren't you?'

'My nose again?'

'No, I mean—' he broke off when he saw the other man giggling. 'Come on!' He laughed through mild exasperation.

'But you make it so easy. Sorry, don't mind me. Just watch your lovely girlfriend.'

He did, leaning against the wall to get comfortable. Karen used long, firm strokes up the thigh, back down, along the side of the knee and across the calf before travelling up again. Over and over she moved the wheel and Dan watched the spikes prick that pale, hairy skin and leave tiny red marks in their wake. Henrietta's breathing hitched. His bound hands twitched. Pre-cum began to dribble from his cock.

Denise whistled softly. 'She's good.'

'Apparently so.' Dan wiped his mouth, surprised to feel his own cock stirring. He shoved his hands into his pockets and imagined the scratchy tickle of those spikes on his own skin.

Karen crawled around and ran the pinwheel along Henrietta's other leg, up the side of his body and into the curve of his armpit. He whimpered and threw himself forward, eyes wide, but she swayed out of reach and kept going. She teased the pinwheel along his arm and into the palm of his trembling hand.

'Shhh,' she cooed in a voice Dan had never heard before. Deeper than usual and heavy with the weight of authority.

Dan choked back a groan. The sight sent a charge through him, tightening the muscles in his gut. He became aware of the depth of his own breathing and the faint whimpers from Henrietta.

Even Karen seemed to struggle, licking her lips and wiping her face. 'Shhh, I'm almost done.'

Tiny beads of sweat popped out on his forehead a marked contrast to the desert like conditions of his mouth. Dan licked his lips but it didn't help. 'Kaz?'

She continued manipulating the pinwheel. Back along Henrietta's arm, over his shoulders and down the far side.

'He's close,' Denise whispered.

'Can I?' Karen spoke quickly, without looking back.

Dan opened his mouth to answer, then realised that the question wasn't meant for him. He looked at Denise, trying to figure out what was going on.

'Of course you can, sweetheart. He deserves it. Try the back of his neck.'

Nodding, Karen wheeled the spikes down again then traced them in a light circle around the base of Henrietta's throat. When she reached the nape of his neck, she used the other hand to push on the vibrator protruding from his ass. He let out a shuddering moan and tossed his head back, shaking in his bonds. Karen ducked aside as an impressive stream of cum burst from the end of his trembling cock to stain his T-shirt. Several drops missed and hit the bed, others, the floor.

Dan gaped. 'Jesus.'

'Oh, well done,' Denise clapped.

Sagging, Henrietta let out huge sigh. He smiled around the gag and grunted something that was probably a heartfelt thank you.

Karen pressed a chaste kiss against his cheek then walked back to Dan. The deliberate sway of her hips reminded Dan of a snake, though he doubted that he was the charmer in this scenario.

'Did I do good?'

With a start he realised that this question was aimed at him. He opened his mouth. Closed it. Opened it again and whispered, 'Hell-fucking-yes.'

Karen's eyes shone. 'Good, because I liked it.'

'Me too,' he breathed.

'Really?'

'I've never seen you act like that before. Fucking hot. Your voice went all . . . *bitch queen*.'

'If you want to hear it again, just ask.'

The idea swelled in Dan's mind. He played with it, turning it over and over, searching for any reason it might be a bad one. 'After Beth—' he began.

She cut him off with a raised hand. 'Sorry, it's okay.'

'No, I mean, after Beth, I didn't think I'd trust anybody to do something like that to me. I like control, giving it up is a big deal. But . . . I trust you.' His stomach gave a pleasant flutter as he recognised the truth in his words.

Denise cleared his throat. 'Would you like to keep that pinwheel? I have dozens.'

Karen clapped her hands. 'Seriously?'

'Of course, sweetheart. Enjoy it.'

She brandished the toy like a trophy. 'Give me your hand, Dan.'

He did at once, and shuddered at the prick of tiny spikes over his palm and fingers. 'That feels good.'

'Now imagine that all over you.' Karen pushed on tiptoe and whispered in his ear. 'Chest. Stomach. Legs. Cock.'

'Kaz . . .'

'Say the word, Dan. You taught me a trick or two, how would you like to be on the receiving end?' She leaned in and nipped his ear.

He winced. The little flash of pain sparked something way down low, woke it up with teasing promises of more to come. He adjusted the front of his trousers, longing for privacy so he could remove them completely. Her breath caressed his neck and he turned toward her to better see his own lust reflected in her eyes.

'You'll pay for that later. I don't remember saying you could bite me.'

Karen gave a cheeky grin and tucked the pinwheel into the top of her corset. 'Sorry, Sir. It won't happen again.'

'It better. But only when I ask for it.' He grabbed her arse and squeezed it to accentuate the point. 'I'm still the master around here.'

She lowered her head, peering up at him through the curtain of her lashes. 'Yes, Sir.'

KAREN

The following morning Karen stretched and rolled over to find Dan staring at her. His gaze followed a lazy path over her lips and nose before landing on her eyes. She grinned, thinking forward to what it would be like to see that every time she woke for the day.

'Good morning,' she murmured.

'Morning. You snore a little, did you know that?'

'I don't.'

'You do. It's cute, like a little grunting kitten.'

Karen snatched a pillow and beat him over the head with it. 'Take that back.'

Dan reared up, grabbing the pillow and hurling it aside. He dived at her and Karen fought back, giggling as he pinned her to the bed, trapping her wrists with his hands. He was so strong. His power lay not only in his desire to control, but his physical strength too. It added a fine layer of icing to the cake that was him as one delicious whole. When his lips pressed down against hers she wriggled against him, opening her mouth to offer her tongue. He sucked it gently, teasing the inner edge of her lip with his. She tilted her hips and spread her legs. Dan sank into the space left between them and she linked her ankles at the small of his back, trapping him in place.

'Morning fuck?' Hope gave her voice a husky edge.

'I considered it.' He released her wrists and trailed his fingers down her arms. When she tried to move a stern look filled his eyes. 'Hands.'

That voice . . . he could tell me to do anything in that voice . . .

She stretched her arms back to their original position, pressing the backs of her wrists against the rumpled duvet.

'Good.' Grinning now, he kissed a hot path down her chest. He lingered over each breast, tonguing each nipple into stiffness before going down. Ribs. Stomach. Belly button.

Each abandoned point on her body melted beneath the flames of passion he left behind. Her limbs jellied until she could no longer move. Not that she wanted to.

Karen watched him reach the faint line of pubic stubble and waited, holding her breath. Dan stared for a brief moment then dipped his tongue into her slit, teasing his way past her outer lips with the tip. She groaned as he lapped her clit, dragging her to the brink of release with so little effort that she felt almost embarrassed by his total hold on her body.

She clawed the duvet. Bucked her hips. 'Yes, yes, please—'

Ecstasy reached a painful peak. Every inch of skin fizzed like a shaken champagne bottle, set to explode the moment the cork popped free.

'No.' At the last possible moment Dan leaned back and dropped a chaste kiss at the top of her pubic bone. 'Go get us some breakfast.' He leapt to his feet.

The order made no sense. Through the mist of pleasure teetering on the edge, she blinked and tried to work it out. 'Wait, what?'

'Cereal and tea please.'

The promise of paradise faded. Her body ached, riding the ebbing waves until they settled down to nothing. Air seared through her lungs as she sat up, panting. 'Tease!'

'Yep. Oh, and toast if they have it. Chop-chop. Check out is at ten.'

Check out. She'd forgotten about the world beyond the walls of Sugar Dust. It seemed like the cage beneath the bed, condoms on demand, and porn on every channel was the real world, while PhDs, bills, and irritating family worries were the dream.

'I don't want to leave. It's great here.'

'We'll come back.'

'When? Can it be soon?'

'If I start looking now, maybe in time for Halloween or Christmas.'

Karen grinned. 'Imagine being here for your birthday. Tinsel. Holly. Mistletoe. We could invite Rebecca or Hannah, or both.'

'I thought you didn't like the Library.'

She chewed her bottom lip. 'I don't, but I do. I like having playmates, I just don't want to spend *all* of our time with them.'

'That seems fair.'

'Can we talk about it more at home?'

'Of course we can. Now go get breakfast.'

Grinning, Karen bound to her feet. She tugged on her rumbled pyjamas and hurried down to the Ball Room.

The large area bristled with bodies and chatter. So close to check out time, there were no demos or displays, but some people still wore kink and fetish clothing. The majority had returned to their causal daywear and Karen saw jeans, skirts, and even suits among the crowd.

She snatched a tray and started to pile things onto it, head still in the clouds. In the middle of choosing between Cornflakes and Weetabix, she noticed the volume of surrounding conversation rise to an unusual volume.

Unlike the day before, many tables were empty. Instead guests clustered around the stack of shelves holding the day's offering of newspapers, broadsheets and glossy magazines. She moved closer, trying to decipher the excited snippets of conversation.

'It would have been worse,' one man said.

'I know.' The woman beside him frowned at the colourful pages of a magazine. 'No pictures, which is good. No names. But easy to figure it out, if you know them.'

Karen inched closer, leaving the tray on a table. She reached the newspaper rails and snagged the last paper from the shortest stack. A man to her left tutted and slouched away. She frowned after him. 'What's all the fuss about?'

'No idea.' Henrietta stood close by, munching on a slice of toast. 'Mind if I join you to find out?'

She smiled. 'Sure.'

They sat at an empty table.

Several others, thwarted in their attempts to get a copy, hurried nearer to peer over her shoulder.

'It's in the cultural magazine,' said one woman. 'Somewhere in the middle.'

'What is?'

'An article on kink, BDSM and polygamy.'

Karen rolled her eyes. 'Not another one.'

'No, no,' the woman reached over and began flipping pages. 'Someone came here under cover. They've been "living as a sub" for about six weeks to figure out what it's all about. Like method acting.'

Henrietta drummed his long nails on the table. 'What sort of woman would do something like that? It's not easy if you're not into it.'

'That's just it.' The woman gave a sage nod. 'It wasn't a woman.'

'Seriously?' Karen helped to turn the pages.

'There.' She stabbed the paper with one finger. 'There, see, that's his picture. No one recognises him, but he must have been here. He's written about the rope workshop and needles demo.'

Karen waited for the woman to move her finger then looked at the picture herself. It took every scrap of control she had not to shriek out loud.

Henrietta gasped. 'Isn't that—'

She kicked him in the shin. When he looked her way she gave him a discrete shake of the head.

'Do you mind if I read it?' The nosy woman leaned in again, her hand curling around the magazine.

Karen shoved her hand away. 'Do you mind?' She skimmed a couple of paragraphs and winced as her stomach clenched. With every word she read, the knots grew worse until all thoughts of eating left her mind utterly. She'd never be able to swallow a bite, let alone keep it down.

'Shit. I'm really sorry, Henrietta. I need to show Dan.'

'Of course. See you later.'

With a quick nod, she rolled up the magazine, leapt to her feet and ran.

Back in the room, she found Dan flipping through news channels. 'I hate Sunday TV,' he said. 'Cartoons or politics. Does anybody watch this stuff?'

She waved the magazine. 'Paul wrote an exposé about you and Beth.'

'Excuse me?'

'Look. That's his picture. And here, "My Life as a Submissive Sex Slave." It's all about him and Beth. And you.'

Dan widened his eyes. 'Really?'

'Read it.'

Dan's bewildered look rapidly became one of shock as he read the article. Karen watched his eyes flick back and forth inwardly berating herself for not reading the pages more thoroughly. Each twist of his mouth or flick of his eyebrow made her insides squirm like a bucket of live mealworms.

'How?' Dan didn't look up from the pages. 'I don't understand how he did this.'

'You said he disappeared yesterday.'

'Beth said he had a work deadline.'

'It must have been this. The finishing touches of his article. It's not all about you, but look, here, near the middle. He talks about "a black-clad brute with a feline pet."'

'Every Dom here wears black. It's like a uniform.'

'Dan, this isn't a joke, it's you! Keep reading. The "green haired banshee"? The "ghost of a rough past rising to haunt new relationships"? He even mentioned coming on to me.'

Dan waved her into silence and kept reading. Two minutes later he looked up. 'Did you read this all the way through?'

'No, some woman kept trying to steal it.'

He smiled. 'Seems he's been doing a series on gender identity, sexuality and the social perceptions of BDSM. This is the last one, but it suggests he's done a lot of research.'

Karen fought the urge to grind her teeth. 'Who cares about research? He's talking about you in a national newspaper. This is way bigger than telling Pete. What if someone from work sees it? Or your parents? What if they figure out it's you?'

Dan shrugged. 'I don't see how. He doesn't use any names. Not even online tags. Just vague descriptions. It could be anybody. Though the "woman too honest and loyal to her Dom to even consider my offer," has to be you.'

'He really said that?' Some of the nervous energy flittered away. She stopped, surprised to realise she had been pacing the room.

'Yep.' He laid the paper on the end of the bed and strode over to her. 'It's a very sympathetic article. I'm surprised the editor let it run since this rag usually prints shitty, opinionated, fear-mongering crap. Paul made us out to be normal, loving and respectful people who happen to have interesting sex lives.'

'You're sure? Let me read it.'

'Not now.'

'But Dan—' she stopped when he laid a hand over her mouth.

'It's fine. Stop panicking. Let's get some breakfast.'

Karen took a deep breath. She let it whistle through her teeth and forced some of the tension out of her shoulders. If he wasn't worried, then surely there was no reason for her to get worked up over it.

'Sorry, I left the tray.'

'We'll get another one.'

As Dan took her hand and led her out of the room, Karen thought more about Paul's words. She remembered his rough hands and cold sneer. The calculating look in his eye when Dan explained about permission and the delight during her showdown with Beth at the breakfast table. She smiled.

By the time they got back to the Ball Room, the crowds had largely dispersed. Those who remained, talked loudly about the article.

Denise and Henrietta caught up to them at their table. In place of dresses, both men wore dark trousers and plain, boring shoes. Neither wore wigs, but Denise, surprisingly, had a long mane of silver-grey hair curling down his back in a thick ponytail. Henrietta had a shiny bald patch and looked oddly butch without his make-up.

'I told you I knew his face,' Denise spoke under his breath. 'I've been following this series and I was really looking forward to today's piece. I knew he was going to cover BDSM but I had no idea how he meant to do it. Imagine going under cover.'

'Dedicated,' Henrietta added.

'I'd say so. Are you two okay?' Denise swept his gaze over the pair of them, lingering particularly on Karen.

She nodded. 'Have you read it properly? Dan says it's not that bad. No names.'

'There is *one* name.' Denise rocked back and forth on his heels. A hint of a smile played over his mouth. 'He talks about his mistress, Lady Bee, and how her views don't seem to match those of everyone else he's talked to. Not unkind, you understand, just pointing out that everyone has a different style.'

'He came here to prove we're all like Beth,' Karen bit her lip. 'He wanted to show that it's just about hitting people and having sex whenever you want.'

'Well it's not.' Dan rubbed the back of her neck. 'And he now knows that.'

Denise stuck out his hand. 'It was a pleasure to meet you both, but we have to go. Our train leaves early.'

Instead of taking his hand, Karen held out her arms. He nodded and she dived at him, squeezing his ribs until he grunted and pulled back. She did the same with Henrietta. 'You've been great this weekend. Stay in touch?'

'Of course, sweetheart. I assume we'll find you on *Kink4Life*?'

'Yep, Kaz Kitten and Spanx.'

'We'll find you. Bye Dan.'

Karen watched Dan shake hands with the other two men and smiled even wider. As they walked away, she pushed up to her tiptoes to press a gentle kiss on his lips. He put his arm around her shoulders.

A loud cry from the other end of the room interrupted the tender moment. Beth, dressed in simple jeans and a plain black t-shirt, stared at a copy of the magazine. Her eyes grew wide as she skimmed further down and her body began to shake. Seconds later, she ripped the pages out and shredded them into tiny pieces with her shiny green nails.

'Lying fuck!' she roared, ignoring the excited whispers around her. 'Lying, filthy, scum-bag!' She stomped out of the room without a backward glance and in her wake the room's conversation volume leapt several decibels.

Karen watched her go then closed her eyes, storing the image in her mind for retrieval later. She pressed her lips together, but the smile kept breaking through. 'I guess she's read it.'

Dan took her hand and kissed the fingers, a tender and loving touch. In that moment, Karen treasured quiet, social worker Dan just as much as she adored "Dan The Dom". She smiled at him and cupped his cheek, content in the knowledge that she had a firm claim to both.

"Dan The Social Worker" tugged her in the direction of the food tables. 'I'm hungry. What about you?'

'Starving.' Squeezing his fingers, Karen bounded after him.

*Enjoyed that, did you? ^_^*
Then please . . . read on!

A Word From Raven

HELLOOOOOO SMEXXY READERS
It's Raven here! ^_^

Just thought I'd stop in and say thank you for reading my humble novel. Hope you liked it!

Since you're here, may I ask if you'd be willing to leave a review on Amazon and/or Goodreads? It doesn't have to be an essay – in fact it shouldn't! – just a line or two on whether or not you liked the story and if you'd recommend it.

I'm an indie publisher and reviews from folk like you help me reach the readers *umming* and *aaahing* over whether or not they want to join the party.

If you liked reading this book, chances are, they might too!

Cheers!

Raven Shadowhawk

ALSO BY RAVEN SHADOWHAWK

The Meeting Each Other Series: The Full Story
When Vicki broke up with Malcolm she felt sure her life was over. She knew she would never find another love like the one they shared and her alcohol fuelled birthday party is but one of her coping mechanisms. That night, as she prepares for bed, unexpected company in the form of her best friend Lara, changes everything for her . . . and for the lives of many of her guests.

For the first time, enjoy the full story. Six different couples enjoy their first or most significant sexual encounters with their loved ones. This sizzling collection includes all six stories in the Meeting Each Other series and, for the first time, a secret look into how it all began in a brand new, wholly exclusive story told through the eyes of Lara Joyce.

COMING SOON FROM RAVEN SHADOWHAWK

Slippers & Chains: Second Base
Dan and Karen kick off their new life together with a fabulous party in their new home. The night barely begins before tension arrives, this time in the form of jealous best friends and unwelcomed family members.

Karen, in the face of some life changing news from her mother, seeks comfort through the most effective means she knows; BDSM. But her desire to release her more dominant side clashes violently with Dan's inability to share what he feels to be his and his alone.

Can she prove to Dan that adding another facet to their D/s dynamic will do no harm to their relationship? And can she do it before his jealousy drives a wedge between them that nothing can pry free?

ABOUT RAVEN SHADOWHAWK

Raven ShadowHawk is one face of the author who writes fantasy and horror under a second pseudonym. She is, according to most . . . okay, according to *herself*, the fun one of the pair.

Living in Leicester, UK with her partner (the Funk Master) and twin sons (known as Sprog1 and Sprog2), Raven writes erotica ranging from sensual and romantic to graphic and totally PWP.

Her interests include badly produced porn, chocolate, dressing up (particularly in matching underwear) and shouting at women who wear stupid shoes and/or skinny jeans.

Newsletter: http://eepurl.com/oyKNj
Blog: www.ileandraXraven.co.uk
Twitter: @ileandraXraven
Facebook: www.facebook.com/illyandraven

www.ingramcontent.com/pod-product-compliance
Lightning Source LLC
Chambersburg PA
CBHW021048130626
46552CB00005B/2065